I0584713

Published July 2022
Published by Indies United Publishing House, LLC

Cover art by Danielle Johnston

ISBN: 978-1-64456-490-5 (hardcover)
ISBN: 978-1-64456-491-2 (paperback)
ISBN: 978-1-64456-493-6 (ePub)
ISBN: 978-1-64456-492-9 (Mobi)

Library of Congress Control Number: 2022939226

INDIES UNITED PUBLISHING HOUSE, LLC
P.O. BOX 3071
QUINCY, IL 62305-3071

www.indiesunited.net

i

CHASING THE EDGE

The Cari Turnlyle Series: Book 1

by Leslie A. Piggott

INDIES UNITED PUBLISHING HOUSE, LLC

Leslie A. Piggott

Dedication

To Brad, Abby, and Simon: thank you for always believing in me as I chase my dreams.

Table of Contents

Prologue

October 2019

John Delamont looked at his friend incredulously. He ran his fingers through his dark hair for at least the third time in the last five minutes.

"Bryan, are you kidding me? You made super hamsters? Is this some kind of joke?"

"Laugh all you want, but one day, you'll be saying that you knew me when." Bryan swept his bangs out of his eyes. His dark wavy hair constantly needed to be trimmed, but he rarely made time for it. "Come with me, and I'll show you."

"Do I need protection? Can your hamsters hurt me?" He winked one of his bright, blue eyes at Bryan.

"Dr. Delamont, always a comedian. My hamsters are very well behaved. Now, right this way."

They made their way down the hall to Bryan's lab. It was the weekend, so the building was virtually deserted. Bryan directed John to turn to the right and unlocked the second door. He flipped on the lights causing both men to blink in the brightness. The back of the room was a wall of cages, each with one hamster inside.

"How many hamsters do you have here? Forty?"

"Precisely, John. I knew you were good at something other than being funny. Now, look at this one." Bryan pointed at a hamster on the far right.

"It's asleep. Wow." John mimed yawning.

"This one over here is from the same litter but has been given a different type of *nutrition*. Watch closely." Bryan pointed at the hamster in the cage next to the first one. The hamster was running in its little wheel, which Bryan had hooked up to a speedometer. The digital screen read nine miles per hour. "Impressive, right?"

"If I had any inkling how fast a regular hamster could run, it might be more meaningful, Bryan."

"The average hamster can run three to six miles per hour." Bryan's dark eyes sparkled with pride.

"What's the secret? Did you make hamster steroids?"

"No! They are certainly NOT steroids. Nothing of the kind. It's pretty complex biochemistry. Are you sure you want me to explain?"

John sighed. "I'll do my best to keep up, Dr. Hartfeld. Lay it on me."

"Okay, so not too long ago, the genes that make fast twitch muscles were identified, as were the ones for larger and stronger muscles, the ones that make you jump higher, etcetera. I was able to identify a gene that helps balance these more powerful genes; it's kind of like a suppressor. I hypothesized that it keeps people or animals from being, well, superheroes, you know?

"I found a way to mute that gene with just a small dietary supplement. This hamster running in its wheel can run this fast for much longer than a regular hamster can run at all. It's stronger and more agile too."

"Why aren't you a gazillionaire then? People would pay a lot of money to have this and be the best in their field. Does it not work in humans?"

"I would never dream of testing it in humans, John, though the gene is the same, so *in theory*, it would behave the same way. However, if everyone is taking the supplement, no one has any sort of advantage. This isn't something I'm studying to get rich. It's like my pet project; pardon the pun. I was just curious if it would work."

"What's the harm in testing it in humans? I'm sure tons of people would be interested. I mean, are the changes permanent, or do you have to keep feeding them the supplement?"

"First of all, it's not permanent. I only give them a very small

2

amount once a month. I found that if I stop, the hamster is very close to *average* again within two months. Testing in humans is so much more complicated, John. You don't know how various metabolism differences might affect someone or if someone has an underlying health condition that hasn't been identified. It could be very dangerous. There are numerous metabolic disorders that go undiagnosed for years in people. No, I won't be moving this over to humans."

"Does it affect their lifespan at all?"

"No, there is virtually no difference. It's fascinating, right?"

"I think it has great potential to be fascinating. Are you at least publishing your results?" He raised his eyebrows.

"No, I haven't published it in its entirety. Too many people out there are too greedy to see this as a gain for the scientific community instead of an opportunity for financial benefit. Well, enough show and tell for today. However, one reason I wanted you to see them was because I need someone that I trust to take care of them while I'm on Sabbatical next spring. I'm going to be a guest lecturer over at Oxford, but I can't take my hamsters, of course. As you quickly observed, this treatment that I give them could be rather dangerous in the wrong hands. I don't allow anyone to administer it from my lab. Would you be able to come by on the first Saturday of every month to give the indicated hamsters their dose? I'll give you a key and make sure you have access to the building."

"This suddenly sounds all top secret, like an undercover government project."

"It's nothing of the kind, John. Please don't be dramatic. Someone else will be taking care of the animals' food and water while I'm gone, but I'd like to continue with the supplement program while I'm away. Everything is set up to record their activities. You just have to add a half teaspoon to the water bottles of each of the cages that have a red dot. Once a month, that's it."

He removed his glasses and cleaned off a smudge with his shirt. "Sure, man. I can do that. Just let me know the dates, and I'll get them into my calendar. Where do you keep the powder? Does it have a shelf life, or will it last the whole semester?"

"It lasts for decades, John. It doesn't change at all. Fascinating, right?"

Chapter 1

February 2025

Curtis Whitham sat at his desk and drummed his fingers on it. He couldn't believe his good fortune in hiring Dr. John Delamont to his staff two and a half years ago. The athletic program was finally starting to see some rewards from all their hard work. They were recruiting the top athletes from every field and earning scholarship money from sponsors as he had never seen before. He had been the athletic director of the university for almost a decade. Three years ago, the administration had hinted that if he didn't start landing some better coaches and athletes, they were going to find a replacement for him. He stroked his blonde mustache, remembering the most recent news article lauding his excellent recruitment of coaches and athletes to the university. The writer had called him handsome and a miracle worker. He couldn't argue, his thick blonde hair was still free of greys, and his physique was virtually identical to his days as a college athlete. He was handsome! Maybe he'd keep this job after all. A light knock on his door tore him from his thoughts.

"Dr. Delamont, thanks for stopping by. Have a seat." He motioned to the empty chair on the other side of his desk. "How are all the athletes doing?"

"They seem to be doing phenomenally, from my perspective anyway. No complaints at all." John lowered himself into the hard, wooden chair, wondering if Coach Whitham would ever upgrade his office furniture. The chair couldn't have been newer than 1970, not to mention the so-called cushion of the seat being avocado green. He tried to adjust his long legs to get more comfortable, but it was no use. He stopped himself from rolling his eyes at his own mental conversation. Whitham was technically his boss.

"Wonderful. What about the new guy, um, Stephen? The hurdler?"

"I just saw him yesterday. Everything looked great."

"Okay, good. I know he was a little hesitant about joining the program. Glad he made up his mind. How many athletes are in the program now?"

"Stephen is the ninth athlete to join."

"Fantastic. Should we look into expanding some more at some point?"

"I would be hesitant to do that. I only have a limited quantity, though I might be able to get more at some point. We don't want to start rationing it to our original members."

"That makes sense. You've reiterated that they shouldn't talk about it, right? None of them know who the others are?"

"This is starting to sound like *Fight Club*." John joked, then cleared his throat when Whitham glared. "Um no, sir. As far as I know, it's completely anonymous to all the members, and they all understand to keep it to themselves."

"I know it seems like I'm being extra fastidious about asking them to keep silent. Like we told them, it's not a steroid; it's a dietary supplement. It won't show up on a drug screen because it's not a drug. It's not illegal, right? It's just our little edge." He grinned knowingly at John.

"Exactly." John stood up to shake Whitham's hand. He needed to get back to his office.

* * * * * * * * * *

John walked quickly down the hallway back to his own office. Occasionally, the medical trainers would bring someone by his office for a more thorough examination. Each sport had its own trained medical team, but he oversaw the department. He had been in private practice after finishing his residency when the opportunity to work for the university arose. It had been the chance he had been waiting for, ever since his childhood friend, Dr. Bryan Hartfeld, introduced him to those hamsters. Even though his friend didn't realize the full potential of his work, John could help him. After all, didn't he deserve some payment for taking care of those rodents every spring semester for five years? It was too easy to skim a little from the container of powder each time. He tucked it away for a rainy day and that rainy day had finally arrived with his new position at the university. He knew right away that Whitham would be on board with using the powder. The man was so afraid of losing his job, he'd do anything.

John checked his calendar and saw that Andrew Niles was supposed to be coming in for an appointment any minute. Andrew was usually late, so John took his time getting his desk organized for the day. He wondered what sort of issue Andrew was having. All of the athletes in the program were allowed to make appointments with John without going through their team's medical training staff. They just bypassed the system through the messaging app.

"Dr. D. Sorry, I'm late. It's a long walk over here from my business development class."

"Have a seat, Andrew. What can I do for you today?"

Andrew was the starting left fielder on the baseball team and led the team in home runs and RBIs. He broke the school record for most home runs in a season as a true freshman. Whitham had recruited him heavily when he was a high school senior. They finally won him over when he saw how much success their starting pitcher had with the team in his first season. Andrew was stocky, with medium brown hair and dark brown eyes.

"I was wondering how come the deal with this *program* is so hush-hush all the time. If it isn't illegal, why can't everyone know about it?"

John paused before answering. He didn't want to give the

7

young man the wrong idea. "If everyone knew about it, everyone would want to use it. You'd lose your edge, right? Have you been having any issues?"

"No, Dr. D. None at all. I wouldn't even know I was taking it, except that I can swing the bat so much harder now. It just seems like our whole team could benefit from it, you know?"

"I understand what you're saying, Andrew. I do. It's still a new program, so we're trying to keep it small. Maybe one day, we can expand it."

Andrew shrugged. "I know you've got Wiley in this program. I saw the little packet in his bag the other day. Don't worry. No one else saw it. I figured he was one of us. He throws the ball faster than anyone else in our league. It's incredible. He'll go pro for sure."

John grimaced. No one was supposed to know about anyone else. This was another reason why they kept the program small. He hoped that Andrew didn't try to figure out who the others were too.

"You know I can't discuss another athlete's medical background with you."

"I know. I know. I hear you, Dr. D. I guess that's all I needed. You have a good day." He got up and left the office. John tried to push his fears about Andrew's curiosity out of his mind. He needed to get some work done before heading over to the track later today. Their star hurdler was going to be competing in the meet—the first outdoor meet of the season! He was excited to see how much his time would improve on the larger track. He'd made some good marks during indoor, but this would be the true test.

Chapter 2

Cari Tunlyle walked up to the gate attendant with her press pass. She liked getting to cover her newspaper's university sports section. It was fun to meet the athletes, and she never had to pay admission because of her press pass. She had started to develop a good working relationship with AD Whitham too. He always gave her advance notice if there was going to be a new athlete that she should follow. Today, she was hoping to get a good view of a new hurdler named, she flipped through her notes— Stephen Ithaca. He was a true freshman that had some good success during the indoor track season. Cari hadn't gone to any of those meets as her boss preferred she cover the basketball games instead. They had an aspiring student reporter that wrote the copy for the indoor track meets.

Ithaca was expected to win both of the men's hurdles events today. Whitham had hinted that they might throw him into a relay or two, at least that's what Whitham had heard from the track coach. Maybe Cari could snag an interview with him too. She made her way up the stadium steps to scope out the track. Her press pass gave her access to the field too, in case she wanted to take photos. She thought she could get a better one of him from the front row of the stands though. She unfolded her bleacher seat and sat down with her camera bag and notebook, excited for the events to begin.

Cari had wanted to work for a newspaper for as long as she could remember. As a child she would interview her extended family members over the phone and write up articles using her grandmother's old typewriter whenever she went over to pay her a visit. It wasn't just about sharing information; it was sharing the *heart* of the story with her readers. In middle school, she had petitioned her English teacher repeatedly until she let her start a quarterly newsletter for the school. The first year, she had put the entire thing together on her own, but by eighth grade, they had created a journalism club for the sole purpose of learning about creating and editing a newsletter. The editor of their local paper had even come to a few of their meetings, encouraging the aspiring writers to stick with their dreams.

Cari's grandmother always encouraged her to reach for the stars. Of all of her family members, Cari was closest to her grandmother. In college, she had received handwritten letters from her grandmother every week. She still called and talked to her on the phone at least once a week, if not more often. Her grandmother was so proud of Cari's success in the journalism world and told all of her friends about Cari's writing. She even subscribed to the *Brenington Beagle* so she could see Cari's article every week. Cari fingered the delicate, gold locket around her neck. Grandmother had given it to her when she graduated from high school. It had a photo of the two of them smiling next to some sunflowers from when Cari was a child. She wore the necklace every day and was always double-checking that it was still there.

Cari was still relatively new at the *Brenington Beagle*, but her dreams of having a front-page byline had not diminished in the slightest. She knew what it took to get there and was committed to putting in the time. Her parents were always asking if she had made any friends or if she was dating anyone new. *Anyone new? She didn't have time to date anyone period.* This was her first *real* job with a *real* newspaper. She had gotten up early the day her first article was printed and rushed to the newsstand down the street to buy a copy. She knew it was probably over the top, but she had plastered selfies on her Instagram feed with her article up by her face. Eventually, she carefully cut her article from the newspaper and had it professionally framed. It hung on the wall in her apartment.

Her parents were constantly worried about whether Cari was

living a well-rounded life. *Was she going to church? Was she eating healthy? Was she making time for friends? Was she ever going to settle down and get married?* She sighed to herself. There was plenty of time to do all of those things later. Besides, she had friends. Just because she didn't go out with people every weekend, didn't mean that she didn't have any friends. *It has been a while since I've said yes to a ladies' night out.* She tried to remember when the last time someone had called to invite her out for drinks or a movie. She had gone to that work happy hour last week with her co-workers, even if she had left early to read up on the next week's match ups in the sports arena. She wanted to get a head start on her research, and it had paid off, right? She was front and center for the track meet right now. Cari knew her editor was going to be impressed with her efforts today.

* * * * * * * * * *

Stephen Ithaca walked hand in hand with his girlfriend, Marjorie Pryor. They were both freshmen and had been dating for two years. He was so glad she decided to follow him to this university even though she didn't make the track team. They had both run the hurdles in high school, but Stephen had always seen more success. Marjorie probably could have competed at a smaller school, but she wanted him to have this opportunity, and she wanted to be with him too.

"I can't believe the first meet is today! I'm so excited to watch you run again, Stephen." Marjorie exclaimed, squeezing his hand.

"Thanks. I really appreciate your support. It's going to be pretty incredible to run against some of the guys from these other schools. I hope I can keep up." His brown eyes held a look of determination. Marjorie recognized it as his *in the zone* look. As his start time drew near, he'd gradually zone out of the world around him and focus on performing his best.

11

"Keep up? You're going to blow them all away. You had a great indoor season. I wouldn't expect outdoor to be any different." She nudged him with her shoulder playfully.

"I don't want to be over-confident. You never know when your rhythm might get off and before you know it, you've clipped a hurdle and fallen out of contention."

"I know. I know. But that never happens to you. You're gonna be great! I'll be in the stands cheering you on the whole time." She squeezed his hand and let go. They had reached the outside of the men's locker room and had to part ways.

"Love you, babe."

"Love you too."

Marjorie pushed a stray lock of hair behind her ear. She was a little jealous of Stephen getting to run hurdles in college. She loved competing but was happy for him too. He had gotten even better since joining the college team. She knew his practices were longer and more intense than theirs had been in high school, not to mention the extra time in the weight room and with a personal trainer. Plus, he had told her that the university's sports medicine doctor had given him a nutritional supplement that was supposed to maximize his power. When Marjorie had expressed concern, he had dismissed it. *"A doctor swears to do no harm, right, Marj?"* He'd asked her. He promised her it wasn't a steroid; it was just a protein powder. Still, she wasn't sure she would trust it, especially since he'd also told her not to talk about it to anyone else. It was just an edge to help them up their performance. *Sounds a lot like steroids to me,* Marjorie thought.

She found her way to the stadium entrance and showed the gate attendant her student ID. The attendant was obviously an athlete from a different sport that got stuck checking ID cards. She gave him a dollar for her entrance fee and then walked up the steps to find a seat. She wanted to be near the finish line, along the last hundred meters of the race, so that she could cheer Stephen on to victory. There was a young woman with curly chestnut hair and a big camera bag on the front row already. She must be one of the press people—she was in good shape and very pretty. She flashed a bright smile at Marjorie as she slipped past her and sat on the edge of the stadium nearest the finish line.

It looked like the running events were going to start soon. She saw the starter walking towards the line and talking on a radio of some sort. The field events were already underway: the women's high jump was still going as well as the triple jump and pole vault. For late February, it was really a beautiful day. There was a slight breeze that kept lifting her hair back out from behind her ear. She had wavy red hair that she usually kept pulled back in a pony tail, minus that one pesky strand. Her blue-grey eyes squinted in the sunlight. She grabbed her bag and rooted around until she found her sunglasses. Now, she was ready to watch.

*   *   *   *   *   *   *   *   *   *

Stephen tried to shake out his nerves as he warmed up in the infield. He had already made it to the finals in the 110m high hurdles, so now he was focusing on following suit in the men's 400-meter intermediate hurdles. The latter was a stronger event for him; he had more stamina to go with his speed. Plus, it seemed like that nutritional supplement was really making him faster. He had asked Dr. D. a lot of questions about it before agreeing to take it. Dr. D. said it was like hitting the mute button on your muscles when they started to scream that you needed to stop. They just got another boost of energy. He heard the announcer call for the men's 400-meter hurdle entries to make their way to the starting line. It was go time.

Before he knew it, he was lined up in the blocks and listening for the starter to say the call signals. The starter gun went off, and Stephen shot out of the blocks towards the curve and the first hurdle. He was in lane four, which was supposed to be the best place to start. As they made their way down the back stretch, he could tell he was ahead of the other runners, even though they still had another curve to pass. He rounded the curve to the final straightaway and kept his speed steady. Barring a catastrophe, he should easily qualify for the finals now. He had two hurdles left. He focused on counting his steps: one, two, three, kick, one, two, three—

"STEPHEN!" Marjorie shouted from the stands as she watched Stephen collapse onto the last hurdle. He'd been running steady and was well ahead of the other hurdlers when suddenly he went slack and just fell down. The crowd gasped, thinking he tripped on the hurdle, but Marjorie had seen his face. His eyes had rolled back into his head before he went down. She knew at best, Stephen was unconscious. She grabbed her bag and ran towards the stadium steps, but the attendants wouldn't let her onto the track. With tears streaming down her face, she begged them.

"Please, that's my boyfriend who fell. Please, he's not okay. Just let me see him." She struggled to see around them, pleading with her eyes as they held her back.

She watched in horror as the team trainer ran onto the track and tried to get Stephen to wake up, but he didn't respond. She saw him check for a pulse, and then he was shouting, but Marjorie couldn't see or hear anything anymore. She knew Stephen was gone. Something very terrible had just happened.

* * * * * * * * * *

John paced the floor outside of Coach Whitham's office. He was in a meeting with two of the track coaches and they hadn't thought to invite John to join them. He really needed to talk to Whitham! His office door had a small window, making it challenging to stand and try to listen to the conversation. Besides,

John didn't feel like standing still.

He had gasped along with the rest of the spectators when Ithaca hit the track. He vaguely remembered hearing a girl scream right before he saw Ithaca go down. The EMTs had rushed over and tried to do CPR, but it was no use; the kid was gone. Many people were speculating that he must have had an unknown condition, an enlarged heart or something like that. It hadn't been in his medical history! Finally, the door to Whitham's office opened, and the coaches started to file out. Their faces looked as shocked as John felt. Whitham motioned for John to enter and closed the door behind him.

"What did the coaches say?"

"Well, you know the kid's parents were not here. They said that his girlfriend had to call them. I didn't even know he had a girlfriend. Heartbreaking from the sounds of it. The coaches said that the EMTs are guessing he had that hyper-whatever cardio thing."

"Hypertrophic Cardio Myopathy?"

"HCM. Yep, that must be it. I have no idea what that means. They said that people are usually screened for it already at this point in their careers, but you just never know." He paused when his office phone rang.

"Coach Whitham speaking. Yes. Yes. Okay. I understand. Thank you for calling." He put the phone down and turned back to John. "That was the medical examiner at the hospital. They won't do an autopsy unless the parents request it, but they did get an image of his heart."

"And?" John prodded.

"They said that it might have been slightly larger than it should be, but it wouldn't have warranted restrictions for competing, according to the ME."

John sighed. "I think we need to hit pause on the program until we know more."

"What?! Why? They won't detect it in his system. Hell, it's almost been a month since the last dose, right?"

"I'm not worried about getting in trouble, Whitham. I'm worried about causing harm to these kids. My friend was right; this is too much for the human system."

"Hold on, now. Let's not rush any decisions yet. When is the next dose day?"

"Today, they're supposed to come by in half hour shifts, you know, so they don't run into each other. I'll just message them and say it's on hold. It won't be a problem."

"I don't like this, John. Some of these kids have been in the program for two years already. If they were going to have a problem, we would have seen it by now."

"I can't continue it until I know what happened with Ithaca."

"We may never know! What if his parents don't want an autopsy?!"

"I'm sorry, Whitham, but I can't risk it. I just wanted to help get this athletic department back on track. I didn't want to hurt anyone. He DIED, Curtis. I should have listened to my friend. This is all my fault." He turned and walked out of the office without waiting for the coach to reply.

John shook his head as he walked back to his office. He couldn't believe that he might be responsible for Ithaca's death. He replayed the race over in his mind, this time hearing the girl scream as Ithaca crashed down to the track. He hadn't even realized that the young man had a girlfriend. He had been too focused on making better athletes. What a mess he'd made.

He opened his office door and then locked it behind him. He didn't want anyone disturbing him for the time being. He pulled up the app that sent separate messages to each of the athletes in the program. Scrolling down slowly through the short list of names, he found Stephen Ithaca and started to remove him from the list, but figured it could wait. Instead, he opened up a new blind message to go out to the group but clicked the little 'x' next to Ithaca's name, removing him from that message. Then he sent the message to the others that there would be no pick up today. The program was on hold. If you had a question, you could come by the following morning to discuss it. He closed the app before he got bombarded with questions from the other eight.

John kept the container of powder locked in the bottom drawer of his desk. He decided to take it home with him for now. He didn't want anyone to break in to get it or show up and demand it from him. Almost no one at work knew where he lived, so it would be safer at home. He stuffed it into his gym bag and zipped it closed. There was no point in staying here any longer. He was mentally and emotionally exhausted. He grabbed his keys and left the office, locking it behind him.

Chapter 3

C ari looked over her notes from the track meet. She also had a pocket recorder that she'd used for some oral notetaking. She pulled it out to listen to her reactions after Ithaca had gone down. Everything after that had been such a blur. They had continued with the track meet, which felt insane to her, but the show must go on, right? She rolled her eyes and hit play.

"The star, um, Stephen has just fallen onto the track. I can't tell if he tripped. Oh my goodness, the young woman next to me looks like she might faint. No, she's going to try to run onto the field. They'll never let her. She must be close to the athlete. Probably not a sister. They don't look anything alike. The kid is still on the track. It looks like a trainer has come over now. Yes, one of the university's medical staff is kneeling next to him. Oh no, I think... What? I think he's unconscious. I thought he might have hit the hurdle, but it seems like he collapsed and oh! They're trying CPR. There's a lot of chaos. The track coach is running over now. And Whitham is sprinting over. No, no, no. I can't. He's dead. They can't bring him back. They used the AED and now they're starting to clean up. They've brought over a cart with a stretcher. This is heartbreaking. Are his parents here? I don't see anyone that seems to be one of his parents. The young woman—where is she? She's being held back by a friend. The friend is holding her and lowering her to the grass..."

Cari hit stop. She felt sick to her stomach reliving the experience. The anguish on that young woman's face! She must have been his girlfriend. Cari wondered what her name was. The whole thing didn't sit right with her. Didn't they screen athletes for that enlarged heart thing nowadays? She made a note to look up the name of the condition. The rest of the meet had continued under a shroud. It was as though none of the athletes felt like they should really be competing, but what else were they going to do? She had received a pdf of the results in her work email. Otherwise, she might not have remembered that the home team won the meet for the women's and men's teams. Cari wondered what the coach was sharing with his team right now. She had wanted to interview him but decided it would be better to catch him later. She could do a follow up article once they figured out what had caused the athlete's death.

She started on her write up for the track meet but couldn't stop thinking about the young man who had died. She didn't want to just gloss over his death, but was that really a story for the sports section? Maybe this was her chance to show what she could do with a real story. It felt awkward or maybe a bit unethical to try to profit from this tragedy, but would ignoring it be wasting an opportunity? She reached for her locket and ran it along the chain. She decided to give her grandmother a call. Grandmother always had good advice.

"Is that my Cari?" Her grandmother's voice rang through clearly.

"Hi, Grandmother. How are you today?"

"Oh, I'm so much better now that you've called."

"Is something wrong? Are you sick?" Cari asked with concern.

"Oh no, dear. Just happy to get to talk to you. You sound upset, though. What's on your mind?"

"Well, Grandmother, I went to the university track meet today—"

"At Onore University?"

"Yes, at Onore. I was covering the track meet for the *Beagle*. Anyway, part way through the meet, the athlete that was supposed to be the next big thing collapsed in the middle of his race. I thought maybe he'd fallen, or maybe I just hoped that he had, but that wasn't it. That wasn't it at all. He died, Grandmother. The young woman next to me must have known him. I'll never forget the agony in her voice when he went down." Cari paused, unsure how to ask her question.

"How tragic. Now you're wondering if you should write about it—how you should write about it."

"You know me so well, Grandmother. I don't know what the right thing to do is. I honestly think that something else was wrong with this kid. People his age with his level of fitness, don't just collapse and die. Doctors screen athletes for the possibility of that now. This shouldn't have happened and I think there is more to this story than just a tragic death."

"I think you would be honoring him to find out what that is. You are a good and honest person, Cari. Follow your heart; it won't steer you in the wrong direction."

"Thank you, Grandmother. You always know just what to say. I have to go now. I love you!"

"I love you more, sweet girl."

Cari ended the call and started organizing her thoughts. She had a few contacts that could help her learn more about Stephen Ithaca on and off the track. She thought about what her grandmother had said. *Follow your heart.* She felt like her heart was sending mixed messages: one about her dream for a front page, above the fold byline, and another about a tragedy that was unthinkable for the young man's family and loved ones. She would have to remember what the purpose of this story was: to honor Stephen's memory. If it got her on the front page, well, that would be a bonus. Her green eyes danced as she thought of the possibilities.

* * * * * * * * * * *

Andrew couldn't believe it when he got the message from Dr. D. *No powder pickup today?! Was he crazy?* He knew that Wiley Granfor was in the program and decided to call him out on it.

i know ur in the program i want 2 talk

Wiley didn't respond immediately. Andrew wanted to figure out who else was in the program too. Maybe together they could get Dr. D to reconsider. Andrew didn't know how the powder worked, but it definitely worked and he didn't want to lose his edge. He figured that they needed regular doses to keep its effectiveness at the right level. He had his eyes set on going pro one day. Losing any progress could ruin that. He checked his phone again. Why the hell wasn't Wiley answering? Wiley had been at the university a year longer than Andrew; surely, he had figured out some other participants in Dr. D's program. Finally, a message popped up from Wiley.

Baseball program? What?

Andrew groaned. Why did Wiley have to pretend? What a rule follower. He rolled his eyes and sent off another message.

i know u know

meet me at the commons in 5

He grabbed his jacket and headed out the door. Maybe Wiley had some answers.

* * * * * * * * * *

Emma Savol looked at her phone and grumbled under her breath. She had suspected that Stephen was in the program too. This message from Dr. D all but confirmed it. He must be putting the program on hold while they figure out what happened with Stephen. She was still a bit shocked by what had happened at the meet this evening. Prior to today, she had only heard about athletes collapsing on the field; she had never actually witnessed it happen. Normally, she didn't watch many of the sprinting events, but they had started running her event the evening before the meet to help keep things moving. Of course, this meant that virtually no one watched her compete. Sometimes it even felt like the track coaches acted like they were obligated to be there for her. The 10,000-meter run was a long race, but it was still exciting. She still worked hard! Plus, ever since she'd joined Dr. D's program, she always placed in the top three at the meets. Wasn't that worth paying attention to?

Emma ran her fingers through her straight, black hair. She had always been told that she was built like a long-distance runner with her long, slender arms and legs. Her dad used to joke that she ate like a lineman, though. She wondered who else was in Dr. D's little program. She had frequently seen another kid from the swim team leaving the building whenever she was going in to pick up her next powder dose. She hated that word—dose. It made it sound like she was using steroids, which she was NOT. Dr. D had been very clear about that. The powder just helped your muscles work more efficiently; it took away the brakes slowing you down. She hadn't told anyone about the powder. He had also been very clear about that. It was almost like they were helping the scientific community by running a test study here. And the results were damn good. She'd shaved two full minutes off of her 10k time since she'd started participating. It was a miracle worker. Maybe she would make the Olympics in 2028!

But now, Dr. D was at the very least pausing the program. How fast would she lose what she had gained? Would her muscles retain any memory of this state? She tried to remember the swimmer's name; the girl was in her College Algebra class their freshmen year. *What was her name?* Casey. Casey water-something. Ryvers! With a y. Emma had thought it was funny that someone with such an incredible swimming ability had the last name Ryvers. Maybe she could find her in the student directory and see if she knew anything else. She pulled out her phone to look her up.

* * * * * * * * * * *

Derek Menemy paced around the weight room. Why would Dr.

D stop the program? He wanted to go over to his office right then and talk to him. Did he realize that he was putting his scholarship in jeopardy? What if he wasn't able to throw the football as far next season? What if he got cut? He couldn't let that happen. He knew that Alan Debony was in the program too. Dr. D had told them not to try to find out who else was in it. They didn't want it getting around because everyone would want it and so on and so on. Alan was a junior and Derek knew his stats from his freshman year. Granted he was a freshman, but he wasn't nearly as fast as he was now. His forty time had gone down by an insane amount. People thought Tyreek Hill was fast, well, even Tyreek was going to be blown away by Alan Debony. The kid was like greased lightning.

Derek glanced around the weight room and saw Alan over on the squat rack. There weren't a lot of other athletes here on a Friday night, so he decided to risk it and talk to Alan. Maybe they could convince Dr. D to change his mind. Why on earth would he pause such a successful program?

* * * * * * * * * *

Coach Whitham slammed his fist into his palm. Who did John think he was? Taking this program away from him! He could not let this happen. Was it only just this morning that he'd been gloating about how well life was going? How could this be happening? All of the athletes had been required to have an exhaustive physical completed before they could begin with their teams at the university. They should have been made aware if Ithaca had a heart condition! Or any other kind of condition!

This was so unfair. This could cost him his job! He'd put his heart and soul into his work. He'd built all these programs from virtually nothing. He rubbed the back of his neck, trying to release some of the tension in it. He'd be damned if Delamont was going to rob him of this one joy in life. He looked through the list of athletes in the program. Which one of them would be desperate enough to get that powder back for the good of the department? Some of their coaches knew a little bit about the program—not about the powder specifically, of course. They only knew that one or two of their athletes were in a special nutrition program with Dr. Delamont. Maybe it was time to bring someone new into the fold. Whose team stood to lose the most if the program went under? Who would John trust the most? Smiling, he highlighted the phone number of the best candidate. They'd be back on track in no time.

* * * * * * * * * *

Cari had only read about athletes dying in the middle of competition; she had never seen it happen before. She knew that there was some sort of heart condition that had been the cause of the majority of the deaths of young, healthy athletes. *What was that called?* She opened a Google tab and ran a search for sudden death and heart disease in athletes. The first ten results were all articles about something called HCM. Cari was not a scientist, so she skipped the explanation once she figured out that this meant someone had an enlarged heart. The first two articles went on to say that screening for HCM had become standard for all young athletes.

She scrunched up her nose. It seemed unlikely that the school's sports medicine doctors would have missed this diagnosis. She redefined her Google search for sudden athlete death and added the word *causes*. She wished there was a search filter option that she could check for a non-scientific explanation. The list of conditions and diseases all had obscure names that she could barely pronounce, let alone understand. She made a list of a few that showed up more frequently and set it aside for later. She couldn't get too technical in her article or her editor, and more importantly, her readers wouldn't stay engaged. People would want to know why a healthy kid collapsed and died, but they didn't want a complicated science lesson. She needed to call someone who understood these topics and could explain them to her. For now, she would finish her brief write up of the track meet and check in with their student interns about the other sports articles.

Chapter 4

Andrew sat down at his kitchen table to catch his breath. His arms were still peppered with goosebumps from what he'd just seen. He knew that he should have been more suspicious about the text he received last night. It seemed innocent at first. They wanted him to meet with Dr. D. and get him to change his mind about pausing the program. Andrew wanted him to keep the program going too, so he was happy to step up and speak for the group. After learning that the pick-up had been canceled yesterday, he'd put in a meeting request for this morning and Dr. D. had accepted it almost immediately. Andrew's heart lurched. He needed to cancel the request. He pulled out his phone and shakily entered his passcode. He let out his breath once he'd deleted the meeting request. He double checked that the meeting had been deleted from Dr. D's availability calendar before closing the app. That was a close one.

Andrew had never been intimidated by the person who had instructed him to go see Dr. D. After what he saw this morning, he would tread more cautiously around the man. Andrew had never been in any real trouble before, but he had panicked in Dr. D's office. He tried to quickly find the powder and get out of there but failed. He'd probably left his fingerprints everywhere too.

* * * * * * * * *

Marjorie looked in the mirror. Her eyes were still bloodshot from crying all morning. Her freckled face was red and splotchy too. She had met Stephen's parents at the airport last night and taken them to their hotel downtown. Her own parents weren't coming. They wanted her to come home and take a break for a few days. She couldn't leave, though. It felt like abandoning Stephen in some ways. She still couldn't believe he was really gone. He was so healthy and strong. He had his whole life ahead of him! She felt her eyes starting to fill again and shook her head in an effort to make the tears stop. How could this have happened?

Stephen's parents didn't want an autopsy, and since there were no signs of foul play, the ME wasn't going to do one. Marjorie wondered if she should tell someone about the powder that Stephen had been taking. Maybe it caused this. Stephen had been running hurdles for almost a decade and he had never had an issue. They had done a physical to make sure everything was fine; this certainly couldn't have been totally natural causes. She didn't know who to ask or what good it would do. Stephen was dead and nothing was going to change that.

Marjorie sighed and grabbed her hair brush. For once, she wished that she wore makeup regularly so she could cover up some of the splotchiness on her face. Maybe it wouldn't be weird to wear sunglasses all day so no one could see her eyes. She gently brushed her hair and tried to make herself look presentable. She had promised to join Stephen's parents for lunch after they met with the track coach and cleaned out his locker at the gym. Marjorie would have preferred to just lay in bed all day and do nothing. At least it was the weekend, so she didn't have to try to go to class.

Marjorie's roommate, Tiffany, had been so kind last night. She hadn't gone to the track meet, but Marjorie had been coherent enough to ask the person who saw her struggling to get to Stephen to call Tiff to pick her up. Tiff had left her job at the local ice cream joint to get Marjorie and bring her back to their on-campus apartment. She'd filled up the bathtub with hot water and bubbles and ordered Marjorie into it. Tiff had listened to Marjorie share endless stories about Stephen. They had stayed up well past three o'clock eating ice cream that Tiff had brought home from work. Tiff had to work again today, but she'd checked in with Marjorie multiple times to make sure she was okay. She felt really blessed to have such a compassionate roommate.

* * * * * * * * * *

Genevieve Viacorte grabbed her notepad and her recorder. She had just been promoted to detective last year and still felt like a rookie. Her partner, Alex Runimoss was a fifteen-year veteran with their squad. Genevieve appreciated his knowledge and experience as well as his willingness to let her take the lead on their cases more recently. They were headed over to Onore University to investigate a suspicious death. Alex said that campus security had been vague about the details when they had called over to the precinct.

"You ready, G?" Alex broke into her thoughts.

"As ready as ever. Is this about the kid who collapsed on the track?" She asked as she followed Alex out to their vehicle. His tall, broad frame blocked her vision. Alex was every bit as tall as she was short. He held the door open for her.

"I don't think so. They made it sound like it was a teacher or coach or something. Hopefully, no one has touched anything." His dark eyes narrowed. "Those campus police officers have no idea how to handle this."

"Are you driving, or am I?" Genevieve tried to keep him from getting too worked up over things out of their control.

Alex grinned and held up the keys. He had straight black hair that he kept fairly short.

"You think I can fit behind the wheel of this thing after you drove it last? I might get a cramp if I don't adjust the seat before I try to squeeze in." He laughed.

"Very funny. I've never heard that one before." She rolled her eyes and got into the passenger seat. She had taken the car to get gas after their shift ended yesterday, then returned it to the station.

She flipped down the visor to shield her eyes from the sun. Even with sunglasses on, her light, hazel eyes would squint to keep the brightness out as much as possible. "What building are we headed to? You mentioned a coach, so the gym?"

"Yeah, the athletic building. Hopefully, we can find a place to park close to the entrance." Alex put the car in gear and pulled away from the station.

"Did they say what made the death suspicious? Is it related to the track kid?"

"They sounded like they were in shock. I heard someone crying in the background too. It sounds like a mess. I have no idea; I'm pretty sure I heard someone at the station say that the track kid died of natural causes even though it was unexpected." He steered along the road that went through the campus. Several students with backpacks were walking along the sidewalk towards the library, which was in the center of campus. A few blocks later, he parked alongside the curb near the gym.

Genevieve had to almost jog to keep up with Alex's long strides. It was windy today and she was thankful that she'd pulled all her hair into a low bun for the day. When she brushed it out, her dark hair fell well past her shoulders. The wind would have tied it into knots today. She scampered up the steps next to Alex and they entered the building. A campus police officer was waiting in the hallway for them.

"Officers Runimoss and Viacorte?" Genevieve stifled a laugh at the way he said their names. She was certain Alex had not mispronounced them over the phone.

"It's a long o, Roo-nee-mohs. And she's just Vee-uh-cort. Nothing fancy, but we *are* detectives." Alex told the younger man.

"And you are?"

"Officer Cravits. This is my first murder. I mean, we don't know it's a murder yet, right? Sorry. Right this way."

Genevieve caught Alex rolling his eyes after Cravits turned to walk down the hallway. They passed the gymnasium and then made a left into the next hallway. Another campus police officer was waiting outside an office at the end of the hall.

"This is Officer Belinda Webb. She can show you the scene. This is Detective Runimoss and Detective Viacorte." He gestured towards Alex and Genevieve.

The tall, thin woman nodded and pulled out a large ring of keys. She had blonde hair with streaks of grey in it. Officer Webb flipped through them before settling on one and sticking it into the lock. Surprisingly, it worked.

"We kept the office locked after we discovered the body. I knew that we shouldn't touch anything. It's quite obvious that he is dead." She grimaced as she led them into the sizeable office.

Genevieve glanced at the nameplate outside the office as they walked in. *Dr. John Delamont-Sports Medicine Chair.* He didn't sound familiar to her, but she hadn't been on the campus much. She made a note of his name and title.

Genevieve could tell right away that some sort of struggle had occurred in the office. There were papers scattered on the floor, a filing cabinet had all of its drawers hanging open, and of course, there were the man's shoes sticking out from behind the desk. She stepped around to the other side and saw that Officer Webb was correct. There was no doubt that the man was dead. The side of his head had a large contusion and there was a large pool of blood under his head. She looked over at Alex and saw that he was looking expectantly at her.

"Who reported the body? And at what time?"

"It was one of our student athletes, an Anna Flarester. She's on the softball team, she said. She used the phone in the hallway to call us. All the phones have specific extensions so we know where someone is calling from before they mention it. She was pretty shaken up."

"And what time was that again?"

"Oh right, sorry. It was just after seven this morning."

"Where is Ms. Flarester now?"

The officer cringed. "She was really upset. I know that you probably want to talk to her, but she wouldn't calm down. I had her call her roommate to come get her. Don't worry, though! I got the roommate's information. We can call her now and she'll bring her back."

Genevieve spoke up before Alex could berate the poor woman. "In the future, and let's hope this isn't something we ever have to experience again, please keep any potential witnesses at the scene. It's pretty important." She looked over at Alex, who was scowling. "Please call and have her return ASAP."

Officer Webb nodded and excused herself. Alex crouched next to the body. He had on gloves and checked around the body to see if anything might have fallen under him when he landed. Genevieve pulled out her phone to call the ME. They had notified him before they left the station but said they were unsure if it would be necessary for his team to make the trip over.

"The ME is on his way along with a crime scene unit. It looks like this trophy was the murder weapon." She pointed at a good-sized trophy on the man's desk. The trophy consisted of a ring of gold stars around an athletic looking man with his arms raised over head. It had a large, white marble base. Several of the stars were outlined in blood and there was more blood smeared on the base. A small plaque at the bottom read, 'John Delamont, state diving champion 1998'.

Alex stood up and looked at the trophy. "It looks like someone tried to wipe it clean. We probably won't get any usable prints off of it, but let's tell them to dust it anyway. Is our witness on her way back yet?"

Genevieve glanced out towards the hallway and saw that Webb was still on the phone. "Maybe. Looks like she's still talking to them."

"I didn't realize that I needed to tell them to keep her at the scene. Good grief. What incompetence!"

Genevieve motioned to Alex to stop as she saw Webb walking back towards the office. The officer stepped inside.

"Um, Ms. Flarester is on her way back." She grinned sheepishly.

"What else can you tell us about her? How did she look? How did she act?" Alex reeled off question after question.

"Um, she was really upset—"

"You mentioned that. What else?"

"Right, sorry. She was crying and her hair was kind of a mess, I guess."

"Was there any blood on her clothing or her hands? Did she have a rag or a cloth? Someone wiped what appears to be the murder weapon clean." Alex said firmly.

"She apologized, Alex. We can't change the circumstances." Genevieve interjected.

"No, no, nothing like that. She looked like she had just gotten out of bed to come over to meet Dr. D."

"Dr. D?"

"Dr. D. That's what all the kids call him. He's the head sports medicine doctor here. He's very well liked."

Genevieve made a mental note of the nickname. It sounded like the man had been friendly with his students. She wondered if any others would be coming by to meet with him that morning.

"Who did he work with most frequently? Who is his boss?"

"That would be Coach Whitham. AD Whitham. Would you like to talk to him too? I can call his secretary and make you an appointment."

"Just get us the numbers and the location of his office," Alex growled. Genevieve cringed. Yes, the officer had really broken a standard procedure by allowing the student to leave, but there was no need to continue to be rude. Webb exited the office again. They could hear someone wheeling something down the hallway and decided that the ME and his team must have arrived.

Genevieve poked her head out to check. Sure enough, a group of people with a gurney were heading their way. Alex indicated to Genevieve that he'd show them the doctor's office. Behind them, she saw a short, stocky young woman drift into the hallway. She was accompanied by a taller, muscular woman. The taller woman had her straight blonde hair pulled back into a tight pony tail, while the other woman's hair was the stereotype of bedhead. Her dark curls were in a cloud around her head. She was wearing a t-shirt and flannel pajama pants. She was grasping her hands at chest level and seemed to be wringing them in an odd way. The woman who must be her roommate was looking at her friend nervously. It was clear that they were both upset. Officer Webb intercepted them before Genevieve could speak.

"Thank you so much for coming right back. This is Detective Viacorte; her partner, Detective Runimoss is in Dr. Delamont's office right now. They have some questions for you." Officer Webb thanked the roommate and instructed her to wait elsewhere.

"Ms. Flarester—"

"Please, just call me Anna," the shorter woman said softly.

"Okay, Anna. I'm Detective Viacorte, and as Officer Webb mentioned, my partner, Detective Runimoss is in the adjacent office. What brought you to Dr. Delamont's office this morning? Seven o'clock seems rather early for a meeting."

"Dr. D always invited us to come chat with him at any time. He is, *was* really easy going."

"Okay, so what did you need from him today?" Genevieve rephrased the question.

"Well, he has been helping me with, um, my nutrition lately, and I, uh, wanted to check with him about some supplements I take and make sure they wouldn't, um, interfere with the plan he had me on." Anna stumbled through her words a bit.

"Was it common for him to provide athletes with nutrition plans? Wouldn't your coach normally do something like that?"

"Yes, well, yes. Our coach has some recommended dietary and nutrition advice, but Dr. D, well, he's a doctor. He *was* a doctor. How did this happen? I just got a message from him last night."

"You texted with the doctor? That seems rather familiar."

"Oh, not really a text. He had a messaging system that we could use to make appointments. We would request a meeting at a certain time and he would confirm the time, and we'd get a message."

"I see." Genevieve made a note to find the doctor's phone; maybe they could see who else he had planned to meet with in the last twenty-four hours. "How often did you meet with him?"

"Oh, about once a month."

"Were there others that met with him too or how did that work?"

"I mean, I'm sure there are, uh, were, but he was always really good about making sure none of our appointments overlapped in any way. He said that he didn't want our meetings to be public knowledge, like doctor-patient confidentiality, you know."

Genevieve found this a little odd. She noticed that Alex had rejoined her in the hallway. She could tell that he found the young woman's statement a little off-putting too.

"Did you see anyone leaving the building or in the hallway when you got here?"

"Um, I don't know. I might have. I didn't really think about it at the time. I was just trying to keep my appointment with Dr. D."

Genevieve sighed mentally. She didn't think Anna was a viable suspect, but they would have to find out from the ME when he was placing the time of death before they could rule her out completely.

"Okay, thank you for answering our questions. We'll need a way to contact you if we come up with more questions. For the meantime, here's my card if you think of anything else." After writing her contact information onto a form that Officer Webb handed her, the young woman turned and walked down the hallway to where her roommate was waiting.

"Officer Webb, how long was Ms. Flarester gone from here? Would she have had time to change clothes?"

"Oh no. The roommate told me that they hadn't even made it back to their dorm room yet. They live on-campus, just a few blocks from here and were on foot. It couldn't have been more than ten minutes and she is wearing the same, um, outfit that she was earlier."

"Okay, thanks."

They turned back to the office to see how the ME was doing. The crime scene unit had dusted much of the room with print powder. Genevieve could see that the filing cabinet had several usable prints, as did the handles to the drawers. Whoever had been here had been looking for something, but what?

"I'd place the time of death between 6:00 and 6:30 this morning."

Alex turned back to Officer Webb. "Does this building have cameras outside or inside?"

"Unfortunately, no. We have been meaning to install them, but just hadn't gotten around to it yet. It's a fairly old campus, so a lot of things need to be updated, but it isn't really in the budget. The building across the way has some, but I don't know if they pick up the entrance to the gym."

"We'd like to see them, just in case. You never know what we might catch."

Webb nodded and took out her phone again to make another call. "I'll have them sent over to you later this morning." She took the card that Genevieve offered with her contact information.

"We need to speak with Whitham, and what about the victim's phone? Has that been recovered?"

The ME held up an evidence bag. "It's right here. I'm taking it over to the lab. Check back with us later to see what they can find.

We took his laptop too."

"Good. We need to know what he did in the last day or so." She turned back to Officer Webb. "When can we meet with Whitham?"

"Coach Whitham is on his way here now. He said that he would meet you in his office in about fifteen minutes. Is there anyone else we can track down for you?"

"Did Delamont have a secretary or administrative assistant? Who was in charge of his schedule? He's the head of the department, right? Where can we get a list of the other people on his team?"

"Coach Whitham can give you those names, or his secretary can. Each sports team has their own team of trainers and medical personnel. Some have more than others, of course." At that moment her phone rang and she paused to answer it.

Genevieve turned to Alex. "When we meet with Whitham, let's see if he'll give us a list of names of student athletes that were under Delamont's care. Whoever did this had access to the building. They must have an ID card or something that lets them get in—

"Officer Webb—" Genevieve interrupted herself, but Webb was still finishing her phone call. She paused while Webb lowered her phone and looked at her. "Does the building log the IDs of people who enter it? Do you have a system for that?"

"That we do. I can look it up and send it over with the video when I get back to our office."

"Thank you. I guess that's all we need for now. You have my card; let me know if anything else comes up."

"Which way to Whitham's office?" Alex asked.

"He's in room 138. You'll turn back to the right and it's in that first hallway near the front office." She went back to her phone call.

Alex and Genevieve walked back down the hallway toward

Whitham's office. The man should be arriving in the next ten minutes. At the very least, Whitham could get them in touch with Delamont's parents. Genevieve hoped someone knew who the man's friends were too.

* * * * * * * * * *

Whitham sat in his car trying to collect his thoughts. The news of John's death had rattled him. He wondered if it had to do with the death of the track kid, *what was his name again?* If John was dead, what did this mean for their program? *Had he left the rest of the powder in his office? Did he take it home?* Questions swirled in Whitham's mind. He couldn't mention the powder to the police, but what if it was still in John's office and they figured out what it was? Maybe he could find out from them if they'd discovered it. He pulled the keys from the ignition and opened the car door. It was time to do a little investigating of his own.

He entered the building and saw a small woman with dark brown hair and pale, freckled skin standing next to a man who couldn't be an inch under six-foot-six. Whitham prided himself on his own height but felt dwarfed near this giant. The man had light brown skin and dark, brooding eyes. He looked back at the woman but quickly glanced away. She had a knowing look in her eyes that told him despite her size, she was not to be trifled with.

"You must be the detectives that Officer Webb mentioned. Um, Viacorte and Runimoss? I see you've found my office. Let me just get the door unlocked for you." He fumbled a bit with his keys but eventually got the door unlocked. He had to pull a folding chair out from behind the filing cabinet so that everyone could have a seat.

"Don't worry about it; I can stand." The man said. "I'm Detective Runimoss and this is my partner, Detective Viacorte. We just have a few questions for you today." He glanced at his partner, who cleared her throat.

"Mr. Whitham, we are very sorry for your loss. We know losing a colleague can come as a shock."

"Thank you. I still can't believe it. I just saw him yesterday afternoon and now..." he trailed off.

The woman nodded. "You said that you saw him yesterday afternoon? Did you meet with him often?"

"We usually only met once a month unless something came up."

"Did something come up or was this your regular meeting?"

"Oh, um, yes, just a regular meeting." Whitham inwardly cringed. *Would they know that he'd lied?*

"Okay, where were you this morning between 6:00 and 6:30?"

"I'm sorry, am I a suspect? Do I need a lawyer?"

"We just need to rule people out," the woman said gently, tilting her head as if to say, *answer the question, fool!*

"Right. Okay. I was at home, asleep. I usually don't come in until almost 9:00 unless I have a meeting."

"Can anyone verify that?" Detective Runimoss broke in.

"Um, I mean, my alarm system at my house can. I set it before I went to bed and didn't turn it off until I left to come here fifteen minutes ago. I can get you a report from the security company."

The woman handed him a card. "Please send it here. Now, how well did you know Dr. Delamont? Did you consider him a friend?"

"A friend? No, he was more of a colleague. I mean, technically, I was his boss, so I wouldn't really call us colleagues either. It was strictly a professional relationship. I recruited him to join our athletic department a little over two years ago, so I didn't know him very well."

She nodded and scribbled something in her notebook. "Did he have a secretary? Is there someone else we can talk to that might know who his friends were?"

"Well, the whole department shares one administrative

assistant. I can set up a time for you to meet with her. I'm sure she's in the office right now."

"We also need to know which athletes he was working with most closely. The student who found his body mentioned that he was helping her with her nutritional plan? Were there others getting this sort of help?"

Whitham hoped he didn't give away the momentary panic that shot up his spine. *Did this student mention the powder?! Surely not, or we'd all be hosed.* "I'm not sure if I'm at liberty to release those names. Doctor-patient privilege and all." The two detectives stared at him blankly. *What were they thinking?!*

"What else can you tell us about him? Was he well-liked? Was he a reliable employee?"

"Definitely. I heard about John from one of our alumni. He had an injury that required some rehab with a sports medicine doctor. The alum was impressed and so I contacted him about possibly joining our staff. He had a good outlook for our student athletes. He encouraged all of our coaches and medical trainers to be proactive with their teams, you know? They didn't overwork the kids, made sure they knew how to eat healthy, warm up and cool down properly, all of it. Our teams have had a much lower injury incidence since John joined our department. He has been fantastic. Everyone liked John, ahem, Dr. Delamont. Do you have any idea who could have done this? Was there anything in his office...?" Whitham's eyes dropped as he realized what John's death meant for his future, especially if he couldn't find the powder before the police did. He absentmindedly stroked his mustache with his left hand.

"We can't really discuss the investigation with you, sir. What about next of kin?"

"Excuse me?"

"Who does he have listed as his emergency contact? Usually that's a spouse or—"

"John wasn't married. I don't think he was dating anyone either."

"Okaaaay, but he still had to have an emergency contact. Can you look that information up for us?"

"You'll have to get that from the office. Beverly might be able to tell you, but you might have to go through HR."

"Thank you. Again, we're very sorry for your loss. If you think of anything else, you have my card." Detective Viacorte got up from the chair as Detective Runimoss nodded. Whitham wondered what they were thinking when the woman turned back.

"I'm sorry, you mentioned a secretary? Where can we find her?"

"She's in the main office at the opposite end of this hallway." He stood up and pointed them in the right direction. As the two detectives filed out of the office, Whitham wiped at the sweat that had started to form on his forehead. He tugged his polo shirt away from his chest a few times to try to cool off. He hoped the detectives hadn't noticed him sweating. At least the shirt was black, so you couldn't see it getting damp under his arms.

* * * * * * * * * * *

Genevieve followed Alex down the hallway. The athletic director had been hiding something. Maybe multiple things. Alibi or not, he was suspicious. She glanced up and saw Alex was holding the office door open for her. Always the gentleman. She nodded her thanks as she looked inside the spacious office. She wondered why Whitham's office wasn't part of this main office. It seemed like it would be easier to communicate that way. A middle-aged woman was seated behind a large desk with a phone to her ear. She held up a finger to indicate that she would be right with them. She looked like she could cry at any minute. Her short, curly, grey hair was meticulously styled and held in place with what

Genevieve could only assume was whatever replaced *AquaNet* from the 90s. As her head bobbed up and down, her gaudy turquoise earrings followed suit. Genevieve wondered if it hurt to have something so heavy pounding into your head like that. Finally, the woman placed the telephone receiver back in the cradle and looked up at them.

"You must be Detectives Runimoss and Viacorte. Coach Whitham just called to tell me that you would be on your way over. Is it true what he said? Dr. Delamont is dead? Murdered?" Her eyes were wide.

"I'm afraid so, yes." Genevieve looked at the name plate on her desk. *Beverly Simpson*. "Ms. Simpson, how well did you know Dr. Delamont?"

"Please, call me Beverly. I didn't know him too well. I usually saw him on his way in and out of the building, but he didn't need a lot from me. He preferred to make his own appointments and he didn't travel with the teams usually, so I didn't need to do travel arrangements for him either."

"What time do you usually arrive at work, Beverly?" Genevieve asked.

"I get here at seven on the dot to unlock the building. All of the coaches and trainers have their own keys if they need to get in during off hours, of course. But I like to get the place open and ready for all of our athletes right away, even on Saturdays."

"We've heard that they can use their ID badges to buzz themselves in? Is that not the case?" Alex asked.

"Oh, yes and no. You see, some students have clearance to enter to use the weight room during our off hours, you know before class or morning practices, but they have to get special permission for that."

Genevieve's hazel eyes sparkled. "Could we get a list of the students with special clearance?"

"Oh, of course! Let me print that out for you. Surely you don't think that…" She put a hand up to her mouth.

"We just need to know who was here and when. Thank you, Beverly. Could you be sure to include their contact information with the list too?" Genevieve smiled at her.

"We also need Dr. Delamont's home address as well as his emergency contact information," Alex added.

"I can print that out too. Just a moment." She typed away at her computer.

"Did Dr. Delamont have any friends in the athletic department? We're trying to get a sense of who he was."

"Friends? I can't say that I knew. Like I said, I usually just saw him coming or going. He didn't really stop by to chat." She handed them the printouts. "Is there anything else that I can get for you?"

"I don't think so, ma'am. Here's my card if you think of anything else." Alex placed his card on the desk and then turned back to the office doors.

Once they were back in the hallway, he turned to Genevieve. "We need to see if he had his house keys on him. He just lives a few blocks from here, though I doubt he shared that with the athletes."

Genevieve nodded in agreement. "The crime scene guys are probably still here. Maybe they found his keys."

They walked quickly over to Delamont's office and found the crime scene unit putting up yellow tape across the office door. Genevieve got their attention by whistling. All their heads turned her way immediately. She hurried over to them.

"Did you find a set of keys in his pockets?"

"We sure did. Let me find them for you." The evidence tech searched through the manilla envelope and retrieved the keys. "Here you go."

"What about prints? Did you find anything useful?"

"We got a lot of prints. Some on the scattered papers, the desktop, all over the place. Not the trophy though. I'm sure that you saw that someone had attempted to wipe it clean."

"We did. Could you use your digital scanner on those prints? Did you get a name for us?"

"Nah. I mean, we scanned them, but other than your vic, no one's name came up in association with any of them. Whoever they belong to, they touched a lot of things."

Genevieve thanked him and turned back to Alex. "I think we should go to his house next. We can look through the list of students Beverly gave us on our way there." She glanced at the list. It had over 150 names on it; she hoped there was a way to easily whittle it down.

"Did Officer Webb get you the list of ID badges that entered the building in the last 24 hours?" Alex asked her as they walked back to the car.

She pulled out her phone and opened her email app. There were two emails from Belinda Webb. She opened the first one; it had a video file from the camera across the street. The second one had a list of ID badges and what times they had entered the building for the past 24 hours, but there were no names. Genevieve frowned.

"What is it?" Alex asked as he unlocked the car.

"She sent the list of badge numbers, but there aren't any names. Ugh. Oh wait. In the email, she says that we can get the names of which badge is whose from the registrar."

"You know she has access to that herself." He rolled his eyes and got in the car. "I guess we'll add the registrar to our list of people to call, but first, let's go meet his emergency contact. It doesn't sound like the person is a family member to me. Maybe we'll get some real information from them."

"You're right. His emergency contact is a Dr. Bryan Hartfeld. Do you think that's his primary care physician or something?"

"Who knows? Let's give him a call."

Chapter 5

Even though it was Saturday, Cari sat at her desk and looked through the news articles that she had pulled up about Stephen Ithaca. The *Brenington Beagle* would print her article about the track meet tomorrow. For now, she wasn't planning on adding any of her suspicions regarding the athlete's death. She hadn't ever run the hurdles, but she had been a track athlete. She had a good idea of how much improvement was reasonable from one season to the next. Ithaca came from a state that ran the 300-meter hurdles, which was fairly standard for high school. They didn't up the distance to 400-meters until college. She seemed to remember that the high hurdles were higher in college than in high school too, which could slow you down. In high school, Ithaca could run the shorter race in just over 14 seconds, but at his first meet in college, he had cut that down to 13.12 seconds, which was not only faster in total time, but per meter also.

Cari opened a new tab and Googled the Olympic qualifying standard for men's high hurdles. Ithaca was under it already, as a freshman! Her shoulders sagged as she realized that he would never get to experience that level of competition or any competition ever again. It sounded impressive to her—this level of improvement, but she wanted to verify it with someone who would really know. She grabbed her phone and scrolled through her contacts list. *There he is!* She selected a number.

"This is Coach Turbin. This can't be Cari Tunlyle, though. She never calls me," the voice on the other end teased.

"Coach Turbin! It is Cari and I'm sorry. I've been busy. How are you?"

"You know me, same ole', same ole'. I heard you got a big-time job at that newspaper. Congratulations! You're covering the sports section, right?"

"Yes, and I actually have a question for you. I've been looking at some hurdle times and was wondering if you could clear something up for me?"

"I can try. What's up?"

"How much time could an athlete reasonably cut off his high hurdle time when he moves from high school to college?"

"Well, you know that depends. If he was kind of a mediocre athlete in high school, but then took it more seriously in college, he could probably improve a lot."

"What if he was a state champion?"

"Well, that's a different story. A state champion is probably running in the low fourteens, I would guess. They will get stronger with more targeted workouts in college, but they aren't going to improve by more than half a second, I'd say. What's this about, my dear?"

"I can't really say right now, Coach. I just think something isn't adding up."

"Well, if I know you, you'll get to the bottom of it. Now don't be a stranger! Check in with me more than once every three years, ya hear?"

"I'll sure try, Coach. Thanks for your help."

Cari ended the call and made a few notes in her notebook. Ithaca had improved his time by more than a full second. It was probably too thin to turn into a story at this point, but she wasn't out of ideas yet. She wanted to see if there were other athletes on the track team with similar improvements. *But what event? Maybe long distance?* Cari scrolled through the website to find the list of competitors. She decided to start with the women's team. Last year, she interviewed someone who had broken the school record. *What was her name?* She scrolled through the list: *Amanda, Allison, Beatrice, Constance, Dani, EMMA!* That was it, Emma.

Each athlete's name was hyperlinked with their results from various meets as well as where they were from. Emma Savol was from Indiana and ran the 10,000-meter event. Cari opened a new tab and found some articles from Savol's hometown about their track team. In high school, she had only run a 5k. *People usually slow down a bit in pace from a 5k to a 10k, right?* Cari opened a new tab to look at times recorded by other runners for the two events. Sure enough, most runners were about ten to fifteen seconds slower per mile in the longer race. She looked at Savol's high school 5k time and then clicked on her college performances so far. The sophomore had competed in the 5k the year before. *Perfect. Now I don't need to do any extra calculations to convert from one race to the other.* Savol had run a 19:40 in high school. Last year again as a true freshman, she had cut significant time off of her race, placing first in their conference meet with a 16:52. Cari remembered that the coach had decided on a whim to throw Savol into the 10k at their conference meet since she already had success in the shorter race. She won it too, which was when she broke the school record. She ran a 33:14, which was actually a faster pace than the 5k. *She must have run the 10k first or on a different day because that's crazy!*

Cari clicked through some of the other athletes on the track team but didn't find any others with such marked improvement. She still didn't think she had enough for a story, but she knew someone else that could give her a new lead. She had a friend over in the medical examiner's office that owed her a favor.

"Cari Tunlyle, coming to collect on my debts, I'm guessing."

"Oh, Bob, you know me too well. Got a minute?" She said airily into her phone. She and Bob had never dated, but she always thought he might be interested. She figured it couldn't hurt to use that to her advantage.

"Let me just take a walk outside and then you can ask your questions," Bob replied.

Cari listened as he scraped his chair back under the desk. She and Bob had gone to the same college; she as a journalism major while he majored in science. He didn't get an MD but stopped at the masters of science degree instead. He hadn't wanted to be a doctor or a medical examiner, but he wanted to examine evidence and help solve cases. Cari had indirectly helped him land his job by writing an excellent article about his skills for their college newsletter. The local paper had gotten wind of it and decided to run the story too. When a job opened up in the ME's office, Bob's name was immediately recognized. They remained friends after graduating as both got jobs in the same town. She heard the sound of the wind and knew Bob had made it outside.

"Okay, Cari, how can I repay my debt this time?"

"Did you do anything with the Stephen Ithaca case? The hurdler who collapsed on the track?"

"I recognize the name. The parents came by here this morning with his girlfriend. His death was ruled to be by natural causes, so we left it up to the parents as to whether or not they wanted an autopsy. They said no."

"Oh rats. Is there any hint as to what caused his death?"

"Well, yes and no. The ME thought it was going to be HCM, uh, the enlarged heart thing. The rest of us were kind of skeptical about that since they screen all the kids really closely for that anymore. Because he was curious, he did a quick ultrasound, and the kid's heart was not enlarged. It was virtually normal in size."

"Okay, so that's the no part; what's the yes part?"

"I'm getting there, patience, friend. The parents were pretty upset. They still wanted to know how their son could have died so suddenly if everything looked okay with his heart and he'd always been healthy. The ME offered to do a tox screen to see if there was anything suspicious that might have caused this."

"Like drugs? Don't they have to submit to random drug tests and stuff?"

"I said I'm getting there. Damn. Where was I? Right, the tox screen. Doc ran every test on that kid's blood that he could think of. It was clean. Whatever caused this, we may never know, but it wasn't drugs or steroids, I can tell you that."

"Your *yes* part still kind of sounds like a *no* part, Bob. Any hypotheses on what caused his death? I was on Google earlier—"

"Google is not a reference, Cari—"

"Hear me out. I was looking up causes of sudden death in athletes and came across a whole slew of things I've never even heard of. I can't even pronounce most of them. Maybe he had one of those conditions."

"Without an actual autopsy, there's no way to rule any of those out, Cari. Many of those conditions would require tissue samples and blood tests. The parents said no, so our hands are tied."

Cari sighed. "What about the girlfriend? I'd like to talk to her. Maybe she knows something else."

"Well, you're in luck. I know her name. It's Marjorie Pryor. She's a student at the university too. That's all I've got. Sorry, Cari."

"No, that helps a lot. I think I can track her down."

"There's one more thing, Cari. I'm surprised you hadn't heard about this through the newsroom yet. We have another body, but you didn't hear this from me, okay? The university's sports medicine doctor was found murdered this morning. I can't say anymore. I have to go." He ended the call, leaving Cari with her mouth hanging open.

* * * * * * * * * * *

Alex pulled the car up to a small brick house with grey trim. Genevieve noticed that the paint was cracked on the trim and the yard was mostly devoid of grass. Several overgrown bushes sat below the front windows. She looked at the set of keys that the CSU team had given them and debated about which one worked for the front door.

"Just try one already," Alex said to her with an irritated tone.

She shoved a key into the lock and turned it. "Success!" The door opened with a lever-type mechanism rather than having a knob below the dead bolt. "Just like Officer Webb, I got it on the first try."

"Yeah, yeah. Congrats, you found the house key," Alex mumbled. "Do you have any fingerprint kits on you? We should probably check that handle before we barge in."

Genevieve pulled a kit from her bag and dusted the handle. It was completely clean, even the lever didn't have a print. "No prints. Did someone wipe it clean?"

"Possibly, or it's kind of chilly this morning. Maybe he wore gloves and didn't leave any prints. Let's go inside and see if the place is wrecked or what."

They stepped inside after putting on booties and gloves so as not to disturb any possible evidence. However, the interior looked untouched. They could see the kitchen from the entryway. A coffee cup sat near the sink and a newspaper was unfolded on the kitchen table. The house seemed lived in, but it didn't appear that anyone had rifled through the doctor's belongings, or if they had, they had been very careful not to make a mess.

"I feel like this is a dead end, Gen," Alex said.

"I agree. We should probably have CSU go over it though, right?"

"For now, let's just lock it back up and put a seal on the door. If the evidence brings us back here, the prints aren't going anywhere, right? Let's call the emergency contact. Maybe they're a close enough friend that they could tell us if anything is missing here."

"I don't know, Alex. I think we have to have CSU dust this place for prints. Maybe we'll get lucky."

"I think it's a long shot, especially when nothing is out of place.

It's been what? Three hours since Delamont was killed?"

"Thereabout."

"I think it's unlikely that someone killed him and then drove over here at the risk of being seen in broad daylight."

"Right. Speaking of, let's get some street cops over here to interview the neighbors. Maybe they saw something."

"I feel like you're hearing my words in a way that I am not saying them."

"Oh, I hear what you're saying, old man. I just think you're wrong. No such thing as too much evidence!"

Alex groaned. "LT is not going to approve this. He's going to make us do it. You know that, right?"

"You're probably right on that one. I'll put in a call and see what shakes out. We can always come back this afternoon." She smiled sweetly at him.

* * * * * * * * * *

Bryan Hartfeld lived fairly close to the university, but on the opposite side of the campus from Dr. Delamont. They hadn't heard back from the registrar after leaving a message about the ID numbers, so they called Officer Webb for help. Being Saturday, they knew no one would be coming into the office unless it was an emergency. Officer Webb let them know that the registrar could meet them in about an hour. That gave them plenty of time to speak with Delamont's emergency contact, Bryan Hartfeld.

They walked up the concrete steps that led to the front porch of a small, tan, brick house. The flower beds were a bit overgrown, but the yard was otherwise well-maintained. The house had been around for a while and the white trim needed to be touched up in several places. Genevieve suspected right away that this was the home of a single man. They knocked on the door and stepped back. A man who looked to be in his forties answered the door. He was wearing small, round-framed glasses that made his dark eyes look enormous. Genevieve spotted a few streaks of grey in his dark, wavy hair when he swept it out of his eyes. His brown tweed jacket was a little frayed on the cuffs and he had a mustard stain on his collared shirt.

"Are you the detectives who called?" he asked through the screen door.

They pulled out their badges to show him. "Yes, sir. Detectives Viacorte and Runimoss. Are you Dr. Hartfeld?" Genevieve responded, introducing herself and Alex.

"As I live and breathe. Well, come on in." He turned and walked into the house.

The beige carpet in the entryway wasn't quite threadbare yet, but Genevieve could see that it was headed in that direction soon. Hartfeld led them into the living room just inside the front door. There was an old sofa and two mismatched chairs next to it. *It's furnished like my college apartment,* Genevieve thought. She and Alex sat down in the chairs while Hartfeld seated himself on the lumpy sofa.

"What can I do for you today? You said this had something to do with John Delamont?"

"Yes, sir. How well did you know John?" Genevieve asked him.

"I've known him almost my whole life. We've been friends forever, since first grade, in fact. Now, what is this about? Is John in some kind of trouble?"

"Are his parents still living?"

"What? No! What's going on?" Hartfeld started to get agitated.

Alex put his hand on Genevieve's arm, signaling her to be silent. "Sir, we're very sorry to tell you this, but Dr. John Delamont was found dead in his office this morning."

The color drained from Hartfeld's face. "He was what? How is that possible? But why are you here?"

"You are listed as his emergency contact, sir. We were hoping that you could tell us a bit about him. Any hobbies, did he like his job, that sort of thing."

"I'm his emergency contact?! But, dead? And you're detectives? He was *murdered*?!"

"It looks that way, sir. We're trying to get a sense of who he was. Anything you can tell us could be helpful to our investigation."

"Of course, of course. John, uh, John loved his job. He would often meet me after work and tell me all about the new athletes at the school. He loved getting to help them achieve their goals and all of that. John's always been an athlete. I guess you know he was tall. He played baseball and basketball in high school, but his real sport was diving. He was a champion diver in college. Not very many people can do that AND be a pre-med major. He always wanted to help people. He was always the athlete and I was always the nerd. But he was a nerd too; he just didn't let many people know that about him. It would have spoiled his look as an athlete, you know?

"He was a bit of comedian, really sarcastic once you spent some time with him." He sighed. "I have so many memories of him. I can't believe we'll never make any new ones."

"We're very sorry for your loss, Dr. Hartfeld. Did Dr. Delamont ever talk about any enemies or people he might not have gotten along with?"

"No, not that I can think of. Everyone loved John. He was well-liked wherever he went."

"You said that you've been friends for a very long time. Did you go to medical school together?"

"What? Oh no. See, I'm not a *medical* doctor; I have my doctorate in biochemistry. I do research science." His face lit up. "John and I attended the same undergraduate university and were roommates again while he was in med school and I was getting my

52

doctorate. It was good to have a friend who understood some of what I was doing, you know? Most people hear me talk about my research and just glaze over before I'm two sentences in, but John could keep pace for the most part. He even took care of my hamsters for me while I was a guest lecturer over at Oxford for several spring semesters."

Alex frowned. "You have pet hamsters?"

Hartfeld chuckled. "No. At the university—they're part of a little project I keep on the side. I work there too; in fact, I suggested that John apply for the position so we could be in the same town again. He moved back here from the big city almost three years ago now. The athletic director was already interested in him and asked him to apply too."

"How often did you and Dr. Delamont see each other?"

"Oh, I don't know. He would come by my office to make me get lunch every now and then. Sometimes, you know, I get so caught up with these hamsters—"

"We understand. When did you last see him?"

"I'm not sure. I'm not very good with dates, you know? Maybe Wednesday? He might have grabbed me for lunch on Tuesday or Wednesday this past week." Hartfeld shrugged.

"And can you account for your whereabouts this morning around 6:00 a.m.?"

"My whereabouts?! Am I suspect now? John and I were friends!" Hartfeld appeared to be getting angry.

"It's just procedure, Dr. Hartfeld. We have to eliminate every possible suspect. I'm sure you can understand from a logical standpoint, right?" Genevieve explained gently.

"Of course, of course, but I can't really give you an alibi. As I'm sure you've realized by now, I live here alone. I don't have an alarm system. John was virtually my only real friend." A single tear slipped down Hartfeld's face.

"We understand, Dr. Hartfeld. That will be all for now. Here's

my card in case you think of anything else that might help us."
Genevieve got up from the chair. "We'll see ourselves out. In the
meantime, please don't leave town in case we think of something
else to ask you."

As they walked back to their vehicle, Genevieve thought about
their conversation with the man. "He had quite the range of
emotions, didn't you think?" She asked once they were inside the
car.

"I noticed that too. Agitated, almost light-heartedness, anger,
then sadness. I'm not sure what to think of the guy. He didn't really
tell us what he was doing this morning at six, you know?"

"Exactly, he just told us that no one could verify it."

* * * * * * * * * *

Genevieve and Alex sat next to each other with the three lists
of names and numbers. One had all the ID badges that had entered
the building in the previous twenty-four hours, the second had a
list of students who had access to the gymnasium at any hour, and
the last one had a list of badge numbers and their owners. The
registrar had been surprisingly forthcoming with the information.
They hadn't even had to threaten to get a warrant.

"Okay, why don't you read off the numbers that are on the
building entry list and I'll cross-check it with the registrar's list to
find a name. You can write it on the building list. Once we've done
all of them, we can verify that they have access on the list from
Delamont's secretary." Alex suggested.

Genevieve nodded and picked up the first list. "Maybe we
should start at the most recent time and work our way backward?"

"Works for me."

"Okay, 18647259. Scanned the badge at 6:27." She waited
while Alex ran his finger down the list from the registrar.

"Jessica Loster. That's L-O-S-T-E-R."

"Got it. 18765920, that was at 6:22."

"April Davis."

They continued this way for several minutes until they got to the time stamp 5:56 a.m.

"I can't find that number on the list. Read it to me again?" Alex asked.

Genevieve repeated the number for him. "No, it's not on the list. This must be a faculty ID badge. The number was two digits shorter than the others you gave me, right?"

"Yes, that's right."

"This must be when Delamont arrived. I think his badge was clipped on his shirt and visible. Did you get a photo of that or do we need to call the CSU to get a look at it?"

"No, I think I got it." She scrolled through the photos that she'd taken earlier with her phone until she got one with Delamont's torso in it. Sure enough, the numbers matched.

"Okay, Alex, so he was definitely meeting someone at the gym this morning."

"Well, we don't know that. Maybe he got there at six every day to work out on his own."

"True. No one mentioned that. Who could we ask?"

"Call Webb, see if they have a time stamp of when he arrived most weekdays."

Genevieve pulled out Officer Webb's card and dialed the number. After a few moments, she was able to confirm that Dr. Delamont arrived to the building close to 6:00 a.m. virtually every week day as well as some Saturdays.

"Okay, so he might have been meeting someone, but I bet someone knew about his habits. Let's go back to the lists. Who else arrived near that time within five or so minutes either way?" Alex asked.

"No one."

"What?"

"The person who arrived before him on this list was someone the previous evening at 9:30 p.m. The rest all arrived between 6:15 and 6:26—all those names that you just looked up. They were almost all women, right? Maybe two guys? Those women must be coming in for the same sport. They lift together on Saturdays or maybe the basketball team was having an early shoot-around or their team was watching film?"

"It seems like the person must have entered the building with him then, right? I guess we can't rule out someone trying to sleep there and surprise him when he arrived."

"That seems rather pre-meditated though, right? I think whoever did this wasn't planning on hurting him. They swung at him with the nearest object. They didn't bring a weapon."

"That makes sense. Let's pull up the video footage from the other building. Maybe we'll see someone entering with Dr. Delamont."

Genevieve woke up her computer and accessed her email account. She pulled the video file up and clicked the play button. She could see right away that it wasn't going to be very useful to them.

"Did she say this was a new camera? This is terrible quality. It's pretty blurry and it's black and white." Alex rolled his eyes. "How tall was Delamont again? He looked pretty damn tall on the floor of his office."

Genevieve looked through her notes. The secretary had also given them a personnel file on Delamont. She found the correct page and pulled it out.

"Six foot five."

"Damn, that's almost as tall as me! Okay, so let's wind this back to 5:53 and put it on double speed."

Genevieve did as he requested and hit play again. Unfortunately, Delamont had not parked near the camera for the other building, nor did he ever cross into the frame before the clock ticked over to 5:57. In fact, no one was in the video for those minutes at all.

"Officer Webb was right; there's nothing on this. The video is useless to us."

"Let's go see if they have anything off Delamont's phone. Maybe someone called him."

Chapter 6

Cari had to take a few minutes to process what Bob had told her. Two deaths in less than twenty-four hours on the same campus? Surely, there's a connection. She decided it was time to track down Ms. Pryor and see what she knew.

How do I find you, Marjorie? Cari wondered. Usually, she would request interviews with student athletes through their coaches, but it didn't seem like Marjorie was an athlete. Still, maybe the track coach could point her in the right direction. She looked through her contact information for all of the university coaches until she found his name. It was Saturday, so the coach wouldn't be on campus unless there was some sort of training activity or practice that he was facilitating. While she would have liked to talk to him face to face, she figured her best chance of catching him was through his cell phone. She selected the number and waited for it to ring.

"This is Eric Buchanan." He answered quickly.

"Hi, Mr. Buchanan. This is Cari Turnlyle with the newspaper. Thank you for answering."

"No comment—"

"Wait, please. I'm looking for Mr. Ithaca's girlfriend. I believe I sat next to her at the meet yesterday."

"Girlfriend? Wait, Ithaca? You're not calling about...?" He trailed off. "Oh, you mean Marjorie?"

"Yes, sir. Do you happen to have a way to reach her?"

"I'm afraid that I don't, but we have practice today at 10, so you might be able to ask some of the other kids, uh, students if they know her."

"Thank you, sir. I will be there."

"I don't want you distracting my athletes, though."

"Of course not! I will get there early and try to catch them during their warmup stretches. While I have you on the line, I do have a few questions for you about Ithaca himself. Do you have a moment?"

"We've been instructed to direct you to our media specialist. I can give you her number."

"I have her contact information, sir. I was hoping to get a sense of who Ithaca was as an athlete. He was off to an incredible start this year, posting fantastic times during the indoor season. I would love to include a quote from you in my article. Had you ever had an athlete improve so quickly this early in their college career?"

"I will not be party to an article that sullies this young man's name in anyway. If you are insinuating that he was using performance enhancing drugs or steroids—"

"I'm not at all, sir." Cari lied. "I can tell that Ithaca was a special member of your team. I never got to meet him or interview him. Are you the hurdle coach or could I speak with his hurdle coach at practice?"

"We're not going around this track again. You have the media person's number; you can call her. Push me on this, and I won't allow you to speak with my athletes at practice today."

"I understand, sir. My apologies. Thank you for your time." She ended the call.

Cari checked her watch. It was already 9:30. She would have to hustle to get over to the track early. She typed a quick email to her boss, letting him know she was chasing down a story and would return soon. Then she grabbed her notebook and her bag and hurried out to the parking garage almost running into another reporter at the door. *Lionel Cardian,* she scowled. That man must be working the Delamont story. He was ruthless, but she could write circles around him if given the chance. She picked up her pace as she rushed to her car. He wouldn't know about Ithaca, so she'd have the advantage.

* * * * * * * * * *

Genevieve couldn't believe their luck. The messaging app that Anna Flarester had told them about was easily accessed on Delamont's phone AND it had contact information for a group of students he had been working with in a more attentive fashion. There were nine names on the contact list. She had taken five and given Alex the remaining four to contact. They were headed back to the gym now to interview them.

"All nine are coming in?" Alex asked her. "I mean, the four I called said they would be there."

"One of the numbers I called didn't pick up. I double-checked the name though; it's the kid from the track yesterday. It's starting to feel like more of a coincidence. Did the ME make a ruling on his death?"

"I'm not sure. We can call over and ask."

"*We?*" Genevieve joked. "I'll give him a call. Just a sec." She pulled out her phone and called the ME's office.

"This is Detective Viacorte. Was there a cause of death in the Ithaca case?"

"Ithaca? Let me pull up the file." Clicking sounds indicative of someone typing on a computer keyboard rang through the speaker. "Here it is. Natural causes."

"You didn't do an autopsy?"

"The parents didn't want one and there was no sign of foul play. We did a tox screen. Came back clean."

"Do me a favor and don't release that body yet. We need to verify that his death isn't related to the new one today."

"You got it. I'll put a hold on it now. When should I tell the parents it will be released?"

"I don't know. I'll keep you posted. Thanks." She ended the call. "No autopsy, so no real cause of death. They're just saying natural causes."

"Okay, well, let's focus on this case for now. If we find a connection, we'll dig into that some more." Alex parked the car in the same place from earlier in the day. "We still need to check the doctor's car too."

"CSU has it. They brought it in already. He had a separate fob for it." Genevieve told him.

"Did they find anything?"

"No, the only prints in it were the vic's."

Alex nodded and strode up the steps to the gym again. Officer Webb was waiting for them at the entrance. She pushed the door open when she saw them approaching.

"Detectives. I have the student athletes waiting in our media room for now. Cravits stayed in there with them."

"Perfect. Is there a room where we can speak with each of them separately at some point?"

Before Officer Webb could answer, AD Whitham came stomping into the hallway.

"What's this I hear about you interviewing our student athletes?"

"Coach Whitham, the detectives are investigating the death—"

He cut her off. "You can't possibly think that one of our students is responsible? They're practically children! Why was I not consulted on this?"

"AD Whitham, I don't believe we need your permission to conduct our investigation. We need to gather all the information available, and that includes everyone that Dr. Delamont was working with, student or otherwise." Genevieve interjected. "Please step aside."

Whitham looked like he might explode, but a stern look from Alex seemed to stop him cold. "In the future, I would appreciate it if I was kept in the loop regarding any interviews with our athletes."

"You know we can't make any promises like that, sir. They are all adults. If we think you need to know something, we'll make sure you know it." Alex pushed past him and continued down the hallway with Genevieve and Officer Webb close behind.

"Sorry about that. I didn't realize that Whitham, well, anyway, I'll try to keep him out of your hair if I can. As I was saying, the athletes are with Officer Cravits in our media room. You had asked about rooms to interview people separately. Yes, there are some smaller rooms attached to the media room. Will that work?"

"I'll take the women; you take the men," Genevieve said to Alex, who nodded as they followed Officer Webb through the building.

They entered a large room with a podium on a stage and several rows of chairs on the floor. The school's name and mascot were emblazoned on the wall behind the podium. Eight students were seated in the chairs while Officer Cravits sat in another chair up on the stage.

"Go Bobcats," Genevieve said, smiling, earning some grins from the students. She spotted Anna right away but wasn't sure who the others were.

"Excuse me? Is this going to take long? I'm supposed to be at track practice right now," a slender young woman spoke up from near the back.

"We'll make it as quick as possible," Genevieve told her. "I'm Detective Viacorte, and this is Detective Runimoss. We found your names in a contact list belonging to Dr. John Delamont. As you probably know by now, Dr. Delamont was found murdered this morning in his office." She watched the eight students for a response, but they all seemed to be aware of it already. "We would like to speak with you about your interactions with the doctor. Anything you might know could be helpful, so please don't hold back." Genevieve caught movement out of the corner of her eye and glanced through the glass doors to see another young woman in jeans and a sweater walking past the room quickly. She wondered who would be at the gym on a Saturday dressed that way but quickly returned her attention to the matter at hand.

"I'll be interviewing the men in the room behind you on the left side and Detective Viacorte will interview the women in the other room. These will be done individually to protect your privacy." He pointed to the back of the large room. "You can wait here with Officer Cravits until it's your turn." He motioned to Genevieve to lead the way to the smaller rooms.

Genevieve called out the first name on her list. "Emma Savol? You'll be first." The slender woman in the back rose. She was wearing a teal pullover hoodie and running shoes.

"Thank you. I really need to get over to practice." She walked past Genevieve to the room on the right.

The smaller rooms consisted of a table with six chairs around them. Genevieve positioned herself to face the door and indicated that Emma should sit across from her.

"Ms. Savol—"

"Just call me Emma. Please."

"Emma, what kind of help were you getting from Dr. Delamont?"

"Help? I guess you could call it help. He, uh, formulated a nutrition plan for me. It's supposed to help me maximize my potential."

"Did you find it effective?"

"Oh yes. I have been very pleased with his suggestions. My times have really improved with his guidance."

"How often did you meet with Dr. Delamont?"

"About once a month, though he told me that his door was always open. He is a great doctor...was a great doctor."

"You got along with him?"

"I think everyone did. I would see him occasionally at various sporting events. He was really engaged with all of our teams. He cared about how we were doing."

"Can you think of any reason why someone would want to harm him?"

"No. He was the best. I still can't believe he's gone. First Stephen and now Dr. D." She sighed.

"You knew Stephen Ithaca?"

"We were both on the track team. It's not that large."

"Did Dr. Delamont help Stephen with nutrition too?"

"You know, I'm not sure. Dr. D didn't exactly advertise or whatever."

"What do you mean, advertise?"

"That was probably the wrong word. Coach Whitham, the AD?" She waited for Genevieve to nod in recognition. "He referred me to Dr. D right after I got to campus. He said that he'd seen my results in high school and thought that Dr. D could help me get to the next level. I assume he had programs for lots of student athletes."

"The only ones he contacted personally were the eight of you. Well, nine if you count Mr. Ithaca."

Emma winced at the name. "Interesting. Did you have any other questions or can I go?"

"Was it common for the AD to interact with individual athletes?"

"He does a lot of the recruiting, so I think he takes some pride in getting to sit down with each of us that have scholarships."

"You have a scholarship?"

"Yes, several of the track team members are on scholarship. I have a full ride though. It's partly academic and partly athletic. Now can I go?" Emma was tapping her foot on the floor impatiently.

Genevieve thought for a moment. "I think that's all for now. Please take my card and give me a call if you think of anything else."

Leslie A. Piggott

Emma grabbed the card and stood up. "Who should I ask to follow me?"

Genevieve looked at her list. "Jess Loster. I'm not sure I'm saying that right, but she's the only Jess on the list." Emma exited the room and called out the name. A tall female with straight, dark hair stood up. She had angular facial features that complimented her dark complexion and eyes. Genevieve could see that the young woman was muscular even though she had on sweats.

"Hi there. How do you pronounce your last name?"

"Loh-ster. I'm not lost." She grinned.

"Okay, then, Ms. Loster. I just have a few questions..."

And on it went for the next half hour. None of the athletes that Genevieve interviewed knew anything helpful. Each had a scholarship, including one other who had a full ride like Emma did. They all loved "Dr. D" and couldn't believe that someone would hurt him, let alone kill him. She wondered if Alex was having any more luck.

She hoped that she only had to wait a few minutes for him to finish with his last interview. She looked out the room's windows into the corridor and saw the same young woman pass by again. She jumped up to try to get a better look, but the woman quickened her pace and disappeared around the corner. Just then, the door to the other interview room opened and a tall, muscular young man with short blonde hair and brown eyes looked her way as he stepped out of the interview room but quickly diverted his gaze. Alex gathered up his notebook and stepped out of the interview room.

"How did it go for you?" He asked.

"I basically conducted the same interview four times. Everyone loved Delamont, he was helping with their nutrition plans, he was a great person, etcetera. It felt like they were all holding something back, but I don't have a clue as to what that would be."

65

"I got the same vibe from the men. They were all quick to sing his praises and couldn't believe this could happen. Were all of your athletes on scholarship?"

"Yes, all four of them, with half of them having a full ride, though one of those was combined with academic scholarships too."

"They all mentioned that he helped them with their nutrition. I asked one of them if this was code for steroids and he was pretty offended that I would suggest it. He was adamant that it was just healthy, balanced eating."

"So, where does this leave us? Do we even have a suspect?"

"Honestly, everyone I've talked to, save for Beverly the secretary, has been suspicious. They're all holding something back, but what?"

* * * * * * * * * * * *

Whitham stormed out of the building to the staff parking lot. *How dare they?* This was his building, his department. He oversaw the athletes and they went behind his back. He and John had worked so hard to keep these kids apart. It seemed like the hits would just keep coming for their program. He needed to get ahead of this quickly.

He pulled out his phone and sent a text. Maybe he could work this meeting to his advantage after all. It was time to call in another favor. He was still too angry to go back to his office, so he started his car. He'd bought the Jag new off the lot a few weeks ago. It was the nicest thing he'd ever owned and even though it was a bit of an impulse buy, he was still glad that he had done it. It made him feel like he fit in more in his new neighborhood up on the hill. The homes up there were part of a gated community with large lots and big mortgages. He had just barely qualified for the loan necessary to get that house. Part of him still wished that he'd listened to the financial planner and gotten something smaller in one of the older parts of town. He was barely scraping by right now, but he knew that the university would give him another raise as long as the athletic department continued to thrive. Until then, he still had some space on his credit cards.

Chapter 7

Cari had gotten to track practice just a few minutes before the organized warm ups started. Unlike her days on high school track, no organized stretching was happening. Everyone was doing their own thing while chatting with their teammates. Several of the students eyed her warily after she revealed that she was a member of the press. The ones that would talk to her claimed that not only did they not know Marjorie, they didn't even know that Ithaca had a girlfriend. Finally, one of the men on the team admitted to knowing Ithaca's roommate. He took Cari's card and said that he would pass it on to the guy and let him decide if he wanted to talk to her.

She decided to cut her losses and was walking back to her car when another athlete pulled up late to practice. The woman was obviously in a hurry but stopped to talk to her anyway.

"I'm sorry to bother you. I'm with the *Brenington Beagle* and was trying to get in touch with Marjorie Pryor. You wouldn't happen to know her, would you?"

"Marjorie? Oh, you mean Stephen's girlfriend? Yes, I've met her."

"Do you have a phone number for her that you could share with me? I'm trying to write an article about Stephen and don't know a lot about him other than he ran track."

"Sure, let me just pull it up for you."

Cari punched the number into her contacts list quickly. "Thanks so much. I really appreciate it." It felt like luck was on her side. The young woman had Marjorie's number from a group chat she'd saved regarding a team party at the start of indoor season.

Cari hurried over to her car so that she could call Marjorie. It was too windy outside to have a normal phone call. She slipped into the driver's seat and turned the car on. She didn't want to get cold if it was a long conversation. Subconsciously, she tugged on her locket and ran it along the thin, gold chain. She hit send on the number the athlete had given her and hoped Marjorie would answer.

This is Marjorie. Leave a message!

"Ugh," Cari said out loud after she ended the call. "Just answer." Before she could redial Marjorie, her own phone buzzed with an incoming call. Cari didn't recognize the number, but wondered if the roommate was already trying to call.

"This is Cari Turnlyle. How can I help you today?"

"Um, this is Ben. Ben Spivets. My friend just texted me that you wanted to talk about Stephen. He said that you work for the paper?"

"Yes, sir. I am a reporter with the *Brenington Beagle*. I mostly cover the sports section. Ben, I'm very sorry for your loss. How long had you known Stephen?"

"Just since August. Neither of us knew any other guys coming to school here, so we just took potluck on roommates. We actually got lucky, though. Stephen was a great guy. I can't believe he's gone. He was, like, the healthiest person I know, uh, knew, uh...you know. He took great care of himself. Ate healthy, always got enough sleep. How could something like this happen?"

"That's what I'm hoping to find out. You said that Stephen was a healthy eater. Had his eating habits changed at all in the last few weeks?"

"No. Not that I had noticed. He rarely ate any junk, you know? Everything seemed the same to me."

"Did his behavior change at all? I know you've only known him for a few months, but had anything seemed off?"

"Stephen would NOT do drugs, ma'am. He was clean as a whistle. He had his little protein powder or whatever, but—"

"His what?"

"His protein powder. Don't all athletes take protein powder?"

"I suppose most do, yes, but you called it 'little.' Why is that?"

"Oh, you know, it was just in a little package, not a big tub or something. He had a smoothie for breakfast virtually every day, but early on last semester, I saw him put this little packet of powder into it. I didn't want to be living with someone that was doped up or whatever, you know? So, I asked him about it. He said that it was some sort of nutritional supplement from the athletic department. They gave it to him once a month. I had almost forgotten about it until you called. He told me it wasn't a big deal, but that they had asked him not to talk about it with others."

"Didn't that seem a little suspicious to you?"

"You know, now that you mention, it *does* seem suspicious, but at the time, he was so casual about it, I just kind of moved on, you know? It just wasn't a big deal. Do you think this is what killed him?"

"I can't really conjecture at this point, Ben. I'm just trying to gather information and see what doesn't fit." She resisted the urge to say *you know* at the end of her sentence.

"I guess I should have reported it. I mean, what was I thinking, you know?" Ben's voice cracked.

"Whoa, Ben. This is not your fault. We don't even know that the protein had anything to do with what happened to Stephen."

"Can you let me know if you find out anything about Stephen? I still can't believe this happened. I missed his track meet—I meant to be there, you know? But it was Friday afternoon and I came back here to catch up on some reading and before I knew it, I had missed his race. But then, my RA knocked on the door last night. He told me that Stephen had been in an accident and..." Ben couldn't finish.

Cari wasn't sure how to respond. "It is all very shocking. I promise to keep you informed, Ben. Again, I'm very sorry for your loss. You've been a big help. Thank you." She waited for him to respond.

He sniffed and his voice cracked again. "Thank you for investigating. I hope you can figure out what happened to Stephen. I just can't believe that he just died like that, you know?" He ended the call.

Cari wrote *protein powder* with a question mark in her notebook. She wondered which person in the athletic department would have given it to him. She was pretty sure none of the athletes would talk to her about it, but maybe she could try Marjorie again. If Ithaca's roommate knew about Stephen taking a mysterious powder, maybe his girlfriend did too. She hoped if she called again, Marjorie would get curious about the same number calling twice and answer. She hit send on her number again.

"Hello?" An uncertain voice answered the phone.

"Is this Marjorie Pryor?"

"This is she, uh, yes, this is Marjorie." She stammered.

"I'm Cari Turnlyle. I work for the local newspaper—"

"No comment. No. I'm not. No—"

"Please just hear me out. I want to help. I'm sorry for your loss. I think we almost met at the track meet. Um, I was sitting near you on the bleachers…?" Cari let her question drift off.

"Okay, and? How can you help?"

"I would like to meet with you—we could get coffee maybe? Or breakfast?"

"No, I'm not meeting. What is your question?"

"Marjorie, I'm…" Cari struggled to find the right words for *do you know if your boyfriend was using steroids?* "Did Stephen mention anything you thought was unlike him or different recently? Had his moods changed or was anything different?"

"What? Are you accusing him of something?!"

"No! No. I just want to figure out what happened. It was terrible. Again, I'm so so very sorry for your loss. Is there anything at all that seemed off about Stephen in recent weeks?"

"He was Stephen. He was excited about the hurdles, about running in college. He was setting goals for the season—he wanted to go to nationals, you know? He said that...well, it doesn't matter anymore."

"What? What doesn't matter?"

"It's nothing. He had a nutrition plan that he thought was really going to take him to the next level. That's all."

"Nutrition plan? What does that mean?"

"I don't know. It was something he worked out with Dr. D. I can't tell you anything else. I'm sorry. Stephen is gone. Nothing you do will bring him back."

"Wait, please. Did this nutrition plan involve some kind of powder?"

"Powder?" Marjorie paused, but Cari could hear a note of recognition in her voice.

"Something that he got from the athletic department perhaps, or you mentioned Dr. D?"

"I can't, um, I'm sorry. I can't talk about that." She ended the call.

Cari pounded her palm into the steering wheel. *Ugh! I really thought we were getting somewhere. She knows something else.* She thumbed off a text to Marjorie.

I meant it when I said that I wanted to help. If you want to meet and talk about Stephen or anything else, please let me know.

Marjorie did not respond. Cari couldn't help but hear a note of fear in the young woman's voice. She wondered how Dr. Delamont tied into this. She felt confident that Dr. D was in fact, Dr. Delamont. She was certain the deaths were related. She set her phone down and put her car into gear. It was time to do some research on Dr. D.

* * * * * * * * * *

Emma went over the day's events in her head while she did her recovery run with the team. She was still reeling from Stephen's death yesterday, but today had brought about a whole host of challenges. She had been stopped by two people wanting phone numbers while she was trying to get to practice. The newswoman had seemed harmless, but still, Emma felt a little guilty sending newshounds onto Stephen's poor girlfriend. But before that, before she had even gotten out of the building after the meeting with the detectives, another athlete had stopped her in the hall. He'd given her his number and said that they all needed to talk. His name was Andrew Niles and he was on the baseball team. He had said that he knew about the program and it was time that they all got together.

She had kind of shrugged it off since she was in a hurry to get to practice, but now she was curious. Maybe one of the others knew how to continue the program or how to get more of the powder. She was glad she had agreed to give him her number too. They were all in the same boat and could work together to make this right. Even though her legs were a little tired from the meet yesterday, she picked up the pace so that she could check her phone sooner.

* * * * * * * * * *

Cari sat down at her desk and immediately pulled up the archives site for the newspaper. She seemed to remember that Delamont hadn't been with the university all that long. Maybe she could find an article about when he was hired. She typed his name into the search bar, but nothing in the last few years popped up. *Maybe the university has an article on it*, she thought. She went to the school's website and found a link to their newsletter. She searched for Delamont and got several hits, including the announcement that he had been hired as the chair of the sports medicine staff. Cari opened the article and skimmed it.

"...local boy...former high school standout..." She read aloud. *He grew up here!* She kept reading and saw where he mentioned looking forward to spending more time with his long-time friend, Dr. Bryan Hartfeld, who also worked for the university in the Biochemistry department.

She looked Hartfeld up on the list of staff and found his office number. Of course, they didn't list his home address on the university webpage, but Cari had a different directory she could search for addresses and phone numbers. Sometimes, she was even able to dig up unlisted numbers or addresses, but not always. She opened the application and typed his name into it. Hartfeld was a fairly common name, but luckily, he was the only *Bryan Hartfeld* in town. She punched his number into her phone and called him.

"Dr. Hartfeld speaking. Who is calling, please?" A gravelly voice asked her.

"Hi, Dr. Hartfeld, this is Cari Turnlyle. I work for the *Brenington Beagle* and was wondering if you had time to answer a few questions today. I'd prefer to meet in person, if possible."

"Certainly, can I ask what this is in reference to?"

"Well, I'm doing a little research on hometown kids that return and work in their communities and your name came up," Cari responded. *It wasn't completely a lie. She was researching someone who had returned to their hometown to work.* She twisted a lock of hair around her finger absentmindedly.

"Sounds interesting. Could you meet me at my lab? I'm just finishing something up before lunch."

Cari got the building and room number from him and headed back out to her car. *Biochemistry, huh? Maybe he knows about the nutrition program.*

* * * * * * * * * *

Genevieve and Alex were back at the station, comparing notes again. They had eight student athletes on a nutrition program, an athletic director acting suspicious, and a wildly emotional research scientist. They all seemed capable of swinging the trophy at Delamont, even if the scientist came off as a bit of a nerd.

"What are we missing here? Should we interview the AD again?" Alex asked her.

"And ask him what? That he seems to be lying about something, and we want to know what it is? That should work."

Alex groaned. "I know, but they're all hiding something. That whole nutrition program smells fishy too."

"No puns. We agreed." Genevieve rebuked him.

"Oh, come on, that was a good one. Not to mention the eccentric scientist and his *pet* project with the hamsters."

"I can only imagine how long you've been holding onto that one." Genevieve rolled her eyes. "Surely, they keep a record of their drug tests somewhere. We could request the history on these eight athletes."

"Nine, if you count Ithaca."

"Ithaca, right. Did the tox screen from the ME include performance enhancing drugs? You call down there and I'll call Beverly Simpson to request the drug test results." She got up and walked over to her desk so that they could both make their calls without talking over each other.

"Hi, Ms. Simpson. It's Detective Viacorte again. Who would I contact for the results from your athletes' drug tests?"

"Drug tests? What? And please, call me Beverly. Everyone does."

"Surely your student athletes have to undergo random drug testing, both for steroids as well as other illicit drugs?"

"Oh, well, yes, but we've never had an athlete test positive for anything like that. I've worked here for two decades and we've never had that happen. We pride ourselves in that. I can send you the results, but they're all negative, for every athlete, for every substance."

"That's impressive. Sure, go ahead and send them on over. I only need them for eight of your athletes." Genevieve read off their names.

"I'll get those to your email in the next ten minutes. Easy peasy. Can I help you with anything else?"

"Not at this time. Thank you, Ms. Simpson, er, Beverly."

"You're welcome, dear." She ended the call.

Genevieve found it hard to believe that none of their athletes had tested positive for a single drug in two decades, but who was she to argue with Beverly? She wondered if the ME had any useful news for Alex. He was just putting the phone back in its cradle when she walked back to his desk.

"Anything?" She asked him.

"I left a message. The last I heard, his parents didn't want an autopsy, so we might not ever learn the cause of death."

"And, we're back at square one."

* * * * * * * * * *

Cari parked along the curb outside Dr. Hartfeld's building. The man had sounded older than someone in his forties on the phone, but maybe he just had one of those voices. She hoped he would be waiting for her when she got to the door. It seemed to be somehow windier than it had been just an hour ago. Thankfully, she'd wrapped her hair into a messy bun that morning. Otherwise, it would have been a disaster right now. Plus, it was a great place to stash her pencil when she wasn't carrying her purse around.

The wind whipped her jacket open as she walked toward the building. She struggled a bit to button it as she walked along the sidewalk. She glanced up at the entrance to the building. A middle-aged man with dark, wavy hair was looking out the double doors. She waved and held up her press pass as she approached the building.

He opened the doors and let her inside. She noticed that his hair did have a few grey streaks at the temples. His dark eyes stared at her intently through a pair of thick glasses. He was wearing a tweed jacket that looked so old it could have been her grandfather's.

"Ms. Turnlyle, I presume?"

She nodded. "Thank you for agreeing to meet with me, especially on a Saturday."

"Happy to do it. Tell me more about your article while we head up to my lab. I still have a few things to finish up."

Cari had reviewed her ruse to get Hartfeld to talk about Delamont on her way over to the school. She hoped he bought it.

"What made you come back to Brenington?"

"I came back initially to help my sister out with our parents. Dementia runs in our family and unfortunately, they both were showing early signs of it. But, I've always loved the area. I probably would have come back either way."

"I'm sorry to hear about your parents. How are they doing?"

"That's the funny part. My sister and her husband wanted to move to a warmer climate, so they packed up my parents and moved them down to Florida a few years ago. I love it here, so I stayed."

They had ridden the elevator up to the sixth floor. Dr. Hartfeld directed her to go to the right.

"My lab is just down the hallway here. I was just finishing up with my hamsters when you called."

"You work with animals? I read that you were a biochemistry teacher."

"Oh, I am. I also conduct some research with my senior level students."

"I see. What are you researching?"

"We mostly study metabolic pathways, but the hamsters are kind of my pet project."

Cari stifled a groan into a chuckle. What a terrible pun!

"Oh interesting! What do you do with the hamsters?"

"Come on in and I'll show you."

She started to follow him into the lab, but just as she was about to step inside, he stopped short and turned around. She could see a wall of hamster cages behind him. His brow was furrowed and a darkness had entered his eyes.

"What I'm about to show you is unpublished research, so I'll need to see a copy of your article before it gets printed."

"Oh, of course. I would be happy to let you look it over first." She smiled lightly, hoping to ease the sudden tension.

"Perfect. I'm sorry to be so uptight about it, but people get scooped all the time in science. I'm sure, as a journalist, you can understand."

Cari nodded. "Of course, Dr. Hartfeld. I get it."

"I've been studying the metabolic pathways of hamsters and was able to maximize their endurance and strength." He showed her how some were running faster on their little wheels while others were sleeping or eating.

"Like hamster steroids?"

"NO!" Hartfeld whipped around and shook his finger at her. Then he took a breath and calmed down in a snap. "Sorry. But it isn't a steroid. It's just a supplement that enhances the abilities that they already have." He paused when she crinkled her nose in confusion. "It's like the governor on cars that keeps them from being able to go really fast. We have genes in our bodies, as do hamsters, that keep us from going faster or jumping higher or being stronger. This supplement just mutes those genes. Silences them so that the hamsters can run faster for longer. They don't do a lot of jumping, so that's more hypothetical." He said, looking at the hamsters.

"And this is approved for human use?"

He whirled around again. "No! Never! It could never be used in humans. Not without significantly more research. I just wanted to verify that my hypothesis regarding the genes was correct."

"It's never been tested in humans?"

"Of course not. I wouldn't allow it. It could be highly detrimental if you don't know absolutely everything about the person, genetically speaking. That's one reason why I've been hesitant to publish my findings. People are too obsessed with financial gains to see the beauty of scientific study for what it is. They would try to capitalize off my findings and rush the process before we really have a true understanding of the big picture." His face darkened again.

"On second thought, Ms. Turnlyle, I would prefer that you not include my research with the hamsters in your article. The risk is too high."

Cari nodded again. "That's just fine, Dr. Hartfeld. Do you use the hamsters in other aspects of your research here?"

"Oh, of course, my dear, of course. My lab studies many aspects of the major metabolic pathway. Everyone wants to learn how to improve their metabolism these days, right? Thankfully, it's a hot topic, so there's a lot of grant money in metabolism, both from the government and the private sector. We're all trying to win the war against obesity together! We've made several major contributions to understanding how our bodies process food and gain energy with these hamsters, well, not these exact ones. Hamsters don't live forever, of course." He grinned.

"Would it be okay if I included a sentence about your research with regards to improving health and wellness—the fight against obesity, as you said?"

"That would be perfectly okay. I still want to see the article before it's in print though."

Cari wanted to ask him about his relationship with Dr.

Delamont, but was worried that she might blow her cover. He seemed a bit volatile and she didn't want to spike his temper again. She decided that she could always call later with some follow up questions.

"Did you have any other questions for me?"

"No, I think I got everything that I needed. Thank you again. I really appreciate your helpfulness today. Good luck with the hamsters!"

"Can you find your way back downstairs on your own? I'm supposed to escort you out, but no one is here, so who cares?" He shrugged.

"Yes, I'll be fine. Thank you again." She waved goodbye and walked back to the elevator. *I might have just discovered the link between Delamont and Ithaca!*

Chapter 8

"CSU finished at the vic's house. They did get some prints that weren't from Delamont, including a bunch of partials that weren't in the system at all." Alex hung up his desk phone as he spoke to her.

"Did they find any useful prints besides the vic's?" Genevieve asked.

"They sure did. Back in the dark ages, we probably wouldn't have gotten a hit on these because the only prints in the system were from criminals or military people." He winked at her.

"Stop stringing me along and tell me already!"

"Sorry, I'm an old man that likes to enjoy his stories." He looked at her wryly. "Turns out, the university started fingerprinting all of its employees a few years ago."

"Let me guess. Whitham left prints in the house!" Genevieve exclaimed.

"Not just Whitham, but Hartfeld has some prints in there too."

"That *is* interesting. We need to talk to them both again. Whitham has a pretty airtight alibi for the time of the murder, but that doesn't mean he wasn't involved somehow." She frowned. "None of the prints left in the office had a match, though. CSU said that they were all either Delamont or one other person. If Whitham and Hartfeld both have prints on file, then it can't be either of them that left prints in the office."

"Or they wiped all the ones they knew they'd left behind? Ugh. We could conjecture about this all day."

"True and who knows when the fingerprints were left there? We need to go interview his neighbors. Maybe one of them saw something or heard something that can steer us in the right direction."

Alex groaned. "Ugh! I knew you were going to say that."

"It's okay. You don't have to say that I was right. I can see it on your face. I won't even say it."

"Say what?" He furrowed his brow.

"Well, if you insist. *I told you so.*" She smirked and grabbed the car keys off of his desk.

* * * * * * * * * *

Genevieve parked the car in front of Delamont's house. The wind was blowing harder than it had been that morning. She zipped up her jacket to keep the chill out. Alex was taking forever to get out of the car. She started to knock on his window but saw that he was on the phone. She put her back to the wind while waiting for him to finish up. She wished that she'd agreed to stop for coffee on the way over. At least that would have kept her hands warm right now. Alex finally got out of the car.

"That was the ME. Yes, the tox screen included the whole gamut of things. It was all clean. No steroids, no drugs, no alcohol for the track kid."

Genevieve nodded. "I guess we can set that theory aside. How do you want to do these interviews?"

Alex looked down the street. "Luckily, it's a pretty short block, only a few houses on each side. How about you do the interviews on this side and I'll talk to the folks across the street? If you think I need to hear something, give me a shout." He shook his phone at her.

"Will do." She turned and ducked her head into the wind. She had pushed for these interviews, but now that they were outside, she was regretting it. She looked between the houses and noticed an alleyway behind the backyards. Standing on tiptoes, she could see the campus buildings just beyond the homes. Something else caught her eye. "Hey, wait up."

Leslie A. Piggott

Alex turned back towards her. "What?"

"Are those frat houses on the other side of these homes? I think I can see some flags with Greek letters."

"Makes sense. Now that you mention it, I think that is where the row of frat houses begins. The sororities are on the opposite side of campus."

"We should interview them too."

Alex grimaced. "Fine. We'll go over that way after we finish up here." He turned and finished crossing the street.

Genevieve walked up to the first house and rang the doorbell. A small black and white placard read *NO SOLICITING* next to the doorbell. While she waited for someone to answer, she looked in the flower bed to see if the home advertised a home security system. If they had a video feed, maybe it would have something useful. She didn't see any signs near the bushes, though. Before she could get a closer look, the front door swung open, revealing an elderly man with a walker. He scowled at her behind his trifocals and bushy, white eyebrows. Small tufts of white hair sat above his ears, in stark contrast to his shiny bald head.

"No soliciting! Can't you read?" He shouted at her and started to close the door.

Genevieve put her hand out to stop him while simultaneously pulling her badge out of her pocket. "I'm Detective Viacorte, sir. I'm not a solicitor. I'm with the police department. I just wanted to ask you some questions."

"Finally! I called twelve hours ago about those kids behind my house. Music blarin' and kids smokin' pot and who knows what else in the alley. Drinkin', drugs, all of it!" He stuck out his hand. "Ronald Peters."

Genevieve cleared her throat. "Nice to meet you, Mr. Peters. Actually, sir, I'm not here about a party or noise issue."

The man wrinkled his nose and glared at her. "Then what the hell are you doing here?"

83

"Um, as I was saying, I just have a few questions about your neighbor next door. Dr. Delamont? Did you know him?"

"The young dude? I hardly saw him. He was always on his phone. Talkin' on it, drivin' with it in his hand—that's illegal now! He didn't take care of his yard." He frowned.

"Um, yes, it looks like he wasn't into gardening much." She tried a different tactic. "Sir, did you notice anything unusual about him last night or maybe this morning? Did he leave earlier than usual or have any visitors? Anything out of the ordinary?"

"Why? Is he dead or something?"

Genevieve coughed to try and hide the shock from her face. "Unfortunately, sir, your neighbor was found dead in his office this morning. We're investigating his death. Anything you can remember about last night or this morning could be useful."

"I saw him come home last night. Normally, I can hear his speakers thumpin' and bumpin' every night when he gets home. He gets here around seven most nights, but last night I almost missed him getting here. If I hadn't been sitting in the front room here, watching the cars go by, I wouldn't have seen him. He seemed pretty upset about something."

"Do you watch the traffic a lot, sir?"

"Somebody has to do it. These college kids speeding down our alley at all hours and you never know when you might see something useful. I gotta watch for the mail too. Damn porch pirates aren't gonna get my packages *or* my mail." He growled.

"Do you have a doorbell camera then?" She asked hopefully.

"Now what the hell would I do with that? Like I want someone spying on my house with some confounded piece of technology. They would steal my identity with that without me even knowing it. Hell no, I don't have a camera out here. My eyes work just fine, young lady!" He snapped at her.

"Of course, sir. Did you see anyone else come to Dr. Delamont's house last night? Or possibly this morning?"

"I saw you and your partner across the street come by earlier."
Genevieve fought the urge to sigh. "Anyone else?"

"Well now, I don't stay up as late as I used to, so anything after eight o'clock is going to slip past me."

She nodded. "What about this morning? Anything?"

He squinted. "Like I said, I saw the two of you, but I wouldn't have seen anything much earlier than that. Saturday morning bingo. I leave here at 7:30 every week and don't get back until nine o'clock. Sorry." He shrugged.

Genevieve sighed. "Thank you, Mr. Peters. Here's my card if you think of anything else. I appreciate your time."

She looked down the street to see how far Alex had gotten while she was speaking with the crotchety old man. He was already four houses down the block. Either people weren't home right now or they hadn't seen anything. She would never hear the end of it from Alex if they came up empty on their neighborhood canvas. She tugged her jacket around herself tighter and trudged along the sidewalk to the next house. Before she could knock on the door, Alex called her cell phone. She stepped back onto the sidewalk to answer it.

"What's up?"

"I made it to the last house on this side. No one is home. I left my card with a note to call when they get home."

"I thought we'd catch people at home on a Saturday afternoon. Shows what I know."

"I'm crossing over to your side. We can meet in the middle. You talked to that first house for a while. Get anything useful?"

"No, it was a bust. I thought maybe I was going to catch an early break because the guy is a complete Looky-Lou about traffic on his street. He goes to bed early and then left early this morning too."

"No cameras?"

"No, even asking about cameras made him angry."

"Good times. I didn't see anything that looked like a camera on my side, either. To be fair, we don't know that anyone came here in the first place."

"You're right. We don't, but we definitely won't find out if we don't ask! See you in a bit, Alex."

She ended the call and walked back up the sidewalk to the house. Not only did it not have a doorbell camera, it didn't even have a doorbell! She tried to open the screen door so that she could knock on the heavier, wooden door instead, but it was locked. She waited about a minute and started to knock again when Mr. Peters shouted at her.

"Young lady! No one lives there anymore! They moved out years ago, but didn't sell the place. It just sits empty!"

She waved at him to show her thanks and walked back down the porch steps. The next house had a "For Rent" sign in the yard, so she skipped it. Alex was already coming down the steps of the fourth house on her side of the street. She let her head drop. This whole thing had been a bust. Maybe the fraternity brothers would be more helpful. Mr. Peters had said that they were having a party last night. She waited for Alex to catch up to her, then turned to match his pace.

"Mr. Peters, the old man in the first house, was complaining about a frat party from last night. It should be late enough that they would be awake by now, right? Maybe one of them saw something or heard something."

Alex nodded. "I guess it's possible. We'll give it a try before we head back to the station."

Genevieve got in the driver's seat before Alex could beat her to it, and they drove around the corner to the frat houses. The four houses lined a cul-de-sac and had several cars parked along the curbs. She saw a spot in the middle and decided to chance parallel parking in front of Alex.

"Whoa, what are we doing here?" He looked at her

incredulously.

"Learning why I should always be the one who drives," she told him as she spun the wheel around and looked over her shoulder.

"Should I get out to help guide you? This is a pretty tight spot."

She ignored him and concentrated on positioning the car near the curb. Their vehicle had a backup camera, but she didn't need to rely on it to get the car in the spot. Soon, she was pulling forward and putting the car in park. She looked over at Alex with a smug grin on her face.

"Did I get close enough to the curb for you?" She laughed.

"Well done." He slow-clapped as he got out of the vehicle. "I cannot believe you just did that. I didn't think anyone from your generation learned how to drive, let alone park!"

"Hush. We're both millennials and you know it. You're just an elder-Millennial." She laughed and put the keys in her pocket after locking the car.

"Elder-what? Do NOT start with that."

"Oh, sorry. Are you Gen-X, then?"

She looked up at the house nearest them and saw the blinds slip back closed. Someone had been watching them pull up to the house. She nudged Alex.

"Someone's home and awake. We're being watched."

"You saw that too, huh?"

They walked up to the house and knocked on the door. A lanky kid with stringy, blonde hair answered the door. He was wearing a t-shirt with Greek letters that Genevieve couldn't quite remember over a pair of ragged blue jeans. His feet were bare.

"If this is about old-man Peters complaining again, I swear! We did not drive through the alley, and our music wasn't even that loud!"

"Relax. We're not here about your party. We're detectives." Alex held up his badge. "I'm Detective Runimoss and this is my partner, Detective Viacorte."

"Mr. Peters *did* mention a party last night. We were hoping maybe someone here might have seen something useful. Are you familiar with the man who lives in the house on the corner over there?" Genevieve asked, pointing over his shoulder to the left.

"The sports medicine guy? He's nice. Keeps to himself mostly, but he'll wave if he's in his backyard and sees us out back. He never yells at us either. Wait, did something happen to him?"

"Unfortunately, Dr. Delamont was found dead in his office early this morning; Mr. uh, what did you say your name was?"

"Jeremy. Jeremy Halifax. Dead? What?"

"Mr. Halifax. Visitors? Did Dr. Delamont have any friends over regularly?" Alex tried to refocus the young man.

"Oh, sorry. Um, you know maybe? Let me ask Tommy. He pays more attention to things like that than I do. He's our president. Hey, Tommy!" He shouted over his shoulder. "He's awake. Don't worry."

Genevieve heard a muffled shout from the interior of the house, followed by what could only be described as a herd of elephants running down the stairs. She looked over Jeremy's shoulder to try to get a better view of Tommy, but the door was only partially opened into the house. A moment later, Jeremy took a step back and opened the door more, revealing a stocky young man with a big grin. He was shorter than Alex by five or six inches, but probably weighed just as much. His t-shirt was stretched tight across his muscled chest, and his neck was almost as thick as his head. He had short, dark hair and brown eyes. Genevieve noticed that he was also walking around barefoot in the house. He put his hand out to introduce himself.

"I'm Tommy. And you are?"

"Detectives Viacorte and Runimoss," Genevieve said, shaking his hand. "We understand that you knew Dr. Delamont?"

He shrugged. "No more than anyone else here. Why?"

"He's dead." Jeremy whispered, causing Tommy's eyes to grow to saucers.

"Over there, right now?"

"No, sir. Mr. Halifax told us that you might remember if he had any regular visitors over. Anything you can remember could be helpful." Genevieve told him.

"Visitors? Hmm. Well, there was one guy that came over pretty often. I can't imagine that he'd be involved though."

"If you'd let us be the judge of that," Alex prodded.

"Right. Okay. Well," he stammered. "Dr. Hartfeld came over pretty often. He's my biochemistry teacher, though. Oh wait, was Dr. D poisoned?" His eyes got big again.

"Obviously, we can't discuss the details of the case with you. Please try to refrain from conjecturing about what happened. How often would you say Dr. Hartfeld came to Dr. Delamont's home?"

"I mean, probably every week, though sometimes he wouldn't come over for months at a time. They seemed to be good friends."

Genevieve nodded. "When was the last time you saw him over here?"

Tommy looked up as he thought. "You know, I think I saw someone there this morning, but I'm not sure if it was Dr. Hartfeld. I wasn't paying that close of attention. Normally, I wouldn't be up early after one of our parties, but it was my turn to make coffee and we were out. I had to run to the store. I saw a car pulling up to Dr. D's house on my way by."

"And what time was that?"

"Probably 6:45 or so. One of our guys had an early morning practice and woke me up at 6:15 wanting coffee." He rolled his eyes. "Sometimes the officer perks are not all that they're cracked up to be."

"What kind of vehicle was it?" Alex asked.

"Dark sedan. Four-door. I can't really remember much more than that. I was barely awake. I'm sorry."

"That's okay. Was the party last night just at your house or was the whole cul-de-sac involved?" Genevieve asked.

"I thought you said..." Jeremy began suspiciously.

"Oh, sorry. We were going to try to interview some of your neighbors too, but didn't know if they would have been awake this morning or not."

Tommy grinned sheepishly. "Definitely were not awake, ma'am, er, Detective. You didn't hear this from me; I'm not admitting to anything, that is, but the party was over here and over here only. I, uh, helped several of our neighbors to their beds last night. No one was getting up this morning from any of these other houses."

"No one else had the early morning practice?" Alex asked.

"We don't have a lot of jocks in the houses this year. The university asked us to give priority to our rooms based on academic performance; we lost a lot of the athletes that way. Not that the athletes aren't academically gifted or whatever, great guys, all of them. They just have other things to balance, right? Uh..." He trailed off.

"I understand." Alex nodded. "Here's my card. If you think of anything else, no matter how trivial, please give me a call."

Genevieve followed Alex back to the rounded sidewalk. "We might as well try talking to them. We shouldn't just take his word for it."

"Let's split up then. You go right, and I'll go left."

Genevieve walked up the sidewalk to the neighboring house. She had only taken a few steps when a foul odor stopped her in her tracks. Glancing to her right, she saw the source: a funky pile of vomit. She covered her face with her arm and continued past it. *Probably not a good sign*, she thought.

Just as she suspected, she was barely able to rouse anyone to the door. The two kids who answered had bags under their eyes and squinted at her as though the brightness was too much. They had all been snoozing until she knocked on the door. They couldn't remember when they came home, much less whether they saw anyone drive past the house. She thanked them and walked back to the car. Alex was already headed her way.

"Anything?"

He shook his head. "I do not miss hangovers like that. Ouch. That must have been some party."

* * * * * * * * * *

Cari returned to her office to finish her article. She didn't have the evidence yet that backed up her theory that Ithaca had died under suspicious circumstances. Rather than get herself and her paper in trouble, she decided to keep it somewhat vague and wrote that the athlete had died of unknown causes. The murder of the sports medicine doctor would obviously be the front-page story. She wondered if she could get the lead reporter on the story to talk to her. Maybe she could share her theory that Delamont was somehow involved in the athlete's death, which led to his own downfall. She checked the news board to see who was covering it. Her shoulders slumped as she read the name. It *was* that pompous jerk, Lionel Cardian. He would never collaborate; he was such a fool. She needed someone to bounce ideas off, though. And then it hit her. Genevieve had made detective recently. She sent her old friend from high school a text.

Are you working the Delamont case?

Cari tapped her pencil on her desk while she waited for her friend to respond. They had been really close friends before graduating from high school. Then Cari went to NYU to get her journalism degree and Genevieve went to a different school to get a criminology degree. Cari winced, realizing she couldn't even remember where her friend went to college immediately. *Syracuse? No. SUNY Cortland, that was it.* Cari got her master's degree, finishing in five years, while Genevieve went straight to the police academy. It was no wonder she made detective so quickly. She was brilliant. Her phone buzzed with an incoming text.

Cari, why do you ask?

She thought for a moment. It's not like she and Genevieve were best friends anymore, but they did keep in touch and would grab a coffee or a drink now and then. Would Gen share details from the case with her?

I'm doing an article on Stephen Ithaca. Have a theory that the deaths are related.

She waited while the cursor blinked, indicating that Gen was typing something back.

I can't really discuss an open case with you, Cari. I'm right in the middle of it now.

Cari grimaced and tried a different angle.

I learned something today about Dr. Hartfeld that I think you'll find interesting. Give me a chance, Gen.

She hit send and hoped that Genevieve would listen. After a few minutes, she had all but given up when another text came through.

I'll call you later. Can't talk now.

Cari shot her fist into the air. She texted Gen back and suggested their usual spot near the university at 9:30 that evening. Then she went back to finishing up her article for the editor.

* * * * * * * * * *

Genevieve slipped her phone back into her pocket. She could tell that Alex was getting annoyed with her. He probably thought she wasn't paying attention to the case, but she just wasn't sure how he would react to her interacting with a reporter. She was a sports reporter, though, not that creep Cardian. She knew Alex hated Cardian, as did everyone else at their station. She glanced

over at Alex and saw him quickly looking away. He grunted.
"I hope I'm not keeping you from something," he said to her.
"Sorry, Alex. A friend was just texting, wanting to catch up. I think I got her squared away." She hated lying to her partner but didn't know what else to say yet.

He grunted again. "Okay, so the facts that we know: Delamont went to his office a little before six this morning. He made it into the building and to his office. He met with someone, they got into some sort of argument, and his visitor brained him with the trophy. Did he get any calls or texts this morning or the night before?"

Genevieve pulled up the file with the info the techs had pulled off of Delamont's phone. "He made a couple of calls the evening before; there are a bunch of SMS texts last night, but nothing from this morning."

"Let's pull the numbers of those phone calls. See who he was talking to."

Genevieve typed the numbers into their database and waited for the names to pull up. "Well, that's interesting."

"What?"

"He called Bryan Hartfeld last night. Hartfeld didn't mention that. Maybe we should bring him in for some more questioning."

"I don't think we have enough to bring him in yet. He would have to agree to come because we definitely don't have enough for an arrest warrant."

"True, but..." Genevieve paused, wondering if this was the right time to bring up Cari. "Okay, here's the thing. The person who was texting me earlier? That was my friend Cari. She works for—"

"The Beagle. Gen, are you kidding me? You're leaking to a reporter?" Alex hissed.

"No! What? No! She texted me. She's writing an article on Ithaca and thinks the deaths are related. She said that she has some information on Hartfeld that we might find interesting. She's a sports reporter. She's a good person. She won't burn us, Alex."

He glared at her. "I don't like it, but I would like to know what she has on Hartfeld besides that he wasn't exactly forthcoming when we interviewed him. When's the meet?"

"So now you want to come too?"

"No. I didn't' say that. I don't mix with reporters. Period. I'll take their information though."

"Later tonight. We're meeting for a drink."

"Speaking of Hartfeld, what kind of car does he drive? The frat guys mentioned a dark-colored sedan. Could that have been his car?"

Genevieve shrugged. "Why don't you figure out what kind of car he drives while I figure out what Cari knows."

Chapter 9

Andrew paced the floor of his apartment. He had been able to exchange numbers with the other seven athletes after their meeting with the detectives. He'd set up a group message and suggested that they meet at his apartment that evening. After some back and forth about a time that worked for everyone, they finally settled on eight o'clock. He looked at his phone. He wanted everyone to be committed, so he asked each of them to reply with their name and their sport. The eight of them represented six different programs at the university. Andrew checked his watch; they should start arriving any minute now. He started to punch in a reminder text, even at the risk of looking like a tyrant, when someone knocked on his door. He checked the peephole and saw the tall girl who had complained about missing track practice staring back at him.

"You must be Emma." He stepped back to let her inside and put his hand out to introduce himself. "I'm Andrew, obviously."

"I figured," she said, stepping inside the apartment but not shaking his hand.

He tried to casually run his hand through his hair instead of standing there with his hand out. Before he could close the door, two more familiar faces walked up. One was Wiley from his team and the other was someone he'd seen at the meeting earlier that day.

"Hey, Drew. Thanks for hosting this." Wiley gave him a fist bump as he walked past. Andrew tried not to cringe at the nickname. "This is Jess. She's on the basketball team." He gestured to the girl whose dark hair was in braids and tied back behind her head. She had on grey sweatpants with an unzipped hoodie over a tank top.

"Hey, Andrew, right? I came straight from our shoot around tonight. Grabbed a quick shower, so I wouldn't be the smelly one in the room." She grinned and gave him another fist bump.

"Everyone's coming, right, Drew?" Wiley asked, looking around the small apartment.

"That's what everybody said on the text," Emma said from the couch, not looking up from her phone. She had on dark leggings and an oversized sweater. Andrew thought she looked bored *and* irritated.

"I'm sure everyone will be here in the next minute or so. Can I get anyone anything to drink? I only have Gatorade or water, sorry."

"Hey, we're all in season here, right? No problem, man. I'll take some water. Thanks." Wiley told him.

"I brought my own." Emma held up a VSCO bottle.

"Oh wow, is that vintage? I didn't know people still carried those. Cool!" Wiley basically shouted at her, causing Andrew to almost cringe again. Emma just shrugged.

"I'm fine, thanks," Jess said as another knock sounded at the door.

Andrew opened the door and four more people walked in. "Hey, guys. Thanks for coming. I was just getting Wiley a water, does anyone else want anything? I have Gatorade too."

A girl with wild, dark, curly hair and green eyes shook her head no. He tried to remember her name. *Anna!* She had been the quietest person at the meeting. He'd heard from Wiley that she was the one who had reportedly found Dr. D dead in his office. He wondered if she was still in shock.

"I'll take a Gatorade, since you're offering." A muscular looking girl with strawberry blonde hair and blue eyes responded. "I'm Casey. I swim the 'fly."

The last two people to enter introduced themselves as Derek and Alan, quarterback and wide receiver, respectively, from the

96

football team. They both declined Andrew's offer of something to drink. After grabbing a water for himself and Wiley as well as the Gatorade for Casey, Andrew sat down in one of the kitchen chairs that he'd previously moved into the living room area.

"Thanks again for coming, everyone. I thought that we could all benefit from knowing each other, especially now that our program seems to be in jeopardy. Like I said in the text, I'm Andrew Niles and I play mostly left field on the baseball team." Andrew said. Wiley, Emma, and Jess followed his lead and introduced themselves to the four late-comers. Then everyone turned to look at Anna.

"Oh, sorry. I'm Anna. I, uh, I'm a pitcher on the softball team." She gave a little nod.

"How do you propose we get this program restarted? I mean, we all know that Dr. D is dead. He was giving us the powder. It all seemed kind of cloak and dagger. Does anyone else even know about it?" Derek asked the group.

"I guarantee Whitham knows." Emma spoke up and everyone turned to look at her.

"What makes you say that?" Alan asked. His short, blonde hair was spiked up. His brown eyes flared when he spoke.

"Didn't y'all meet with him before you met with Dr. D? He was funneling us over to Dr. D. He *knows*," Emma said as the rest of the group nodded.

"You're right. I did meet with him first before seeing Dr. D for the first time." Jess commented.

"Then Dr. D acted like we were extra elite, chosen for a small program for the best athletes and told us not to talk about it, so that others didn't get jealous or whatever," Derek said.

"But do you think Whitham has access to the powder? He's not a sports medicine doctor. He's not a doctor at all." Jess asked.

"We could ask him. We could go to his office *together* and demand that he make this right. I don't want to lose my

97

scholarship. My parents can't afford this school without it." Derek said.

"I don't think we should do that," Emma said nonchalantly. She set her phone down on her lap.

"What? Why?" Several people asked.

"We're not supposed to know about each other. Going together could scare him into canceling it altogether. We don't really know a lot about the powder. Just that it isn't a steroid or on the banned substances list, right? But what if it's still illegal? We don't want to spook him."

"I agree. We need to keep our knowledge of each other under wraps for now. No one has told anyone else about the powder either, right?" Andrew asked. They all nodded in agreement.

"Good. Like Emma said, we need to be careful with what we know. We can't let word get out about the powder, or we could lose access to it."

"What about Ithaca?" Emma asked. "How do we know that he didn't talk about it?"

"Do we know he was in the program for sure?" Derek asked.

"I saw him once." Everyone turned to look at Anna, who hadn't spoken since introducing herself. She was sitting in the corner of the couch with her legs pulled into her chest. "I had gotten to Dr. D's late one time for the pickup. I thought I could still get there before the half hour window closed…and I did! But he must have been early. He was waiting outside Dr. D's office when I came out. I wouldn't have known it was him until I saw the announcement about the athlete dying. It was definitely him."

"Are you okay, girl? Did someone drive you here? You look a little shook." Casey asked her.

"I'm fine. I can drive. My roommate was hovering over me all day. It's good that I got out. I shouldn't stay for too long though. She might get worried and come looking. I told her that I had a team meeting, which is weird for a Saturday night, you know?"

Her words tumbled out in a quiet manner and everyone leaned in to hear her.

"Okay, so Ithaca was in the program. What do we know about him?"

"Virtually nothing," Alan said.

"I know his girlfriend, well, I have her phone number. Her name is Marjorie." Emma spoke up. "And the other guys on the track team were talking about him today. One of them is friends with his roommate. Ben somebody or other."

"Spivets? I know that guy. He's in one of my business classes." Wiley said. "He leads a study group that I go to sometimes. I could stick around after and see if he knows anything without really asking about it, you know?"

"What about the girlfriend?" Jess asked.

"I bet Ben knows her. He seemed to be pretty good friends with his roommate. I hadn't realized it was the same guy. The study group meets at their, uh, Ben's dorm, in the common area downstairs. The next one is tomorrow night. I can find out some more about her."

"Hey wait. I think I know her roommate. Earlier today, I was at the Starbucks over on Washington and there was this other student there from my calculus class. Tiffany is her name. She was on the phone telling someone about how her roommate's boyfriend died the day before. She was really animated, so it was easy to hear the conversation." Casey told them.

"Are you sure it's the same person? I mean, it would be a big coincidence, I guess, but still, we don't want to go down the wrong path." Andrew asked her.

"I'm SURE. She said that the kid collapsed on the track and died. That didn't happen to anyone else yesterday, did it?" Her blue eyes glared angrily at him.

"Okay, great. We can get to Marjorie through Tiffany. For now, let's leave Stephen's roommate out of this. If he doesn't know anything about the powder, there's no reason to make him suspicious."

"I could always just call Marjorie. She came to a couple of the track team parties, so she is an acquaintance." Emma offered. "That way we don't have to include Tiffany unless Marjorie won't talk to me."

"I agree with Emma. Let's start there and see where it leads. The fewer people we pull into this, the better." Alan said.

The rest of the group nodded their heads, agreeing with Alan. They needed to keep a lid on the information or risk losing the program altogether. Andrew started to adjourn the meeting when Derek stood up.

"What was your take on the detectives that talked to us today?" Derek asked. "I don't think our guy knows anything about the supplement. He asked about the nutrition program but never said anything about the powder. Neither did I, of course."

"The hazel-eyed beauty we spoke with didn't know about it either." Jess spoke up. "Or that's my impression. She never mentioned it. They know we're all in this nutrition program, but to them it's like dietary management, nothing more."

"Hazel-eyed beauty? Excuse me?" Wiley teased.

"Hey, I'm just saying, the woman has pretty eyes and a pretty face." Jess defended herself. "Don't be jealous that you had to get questioned by the huge man. That guy could put you in your place."

"Ahem." Andrew cleared his throat. "Any other questions? If not, then let's keep in touch via text as much as possible. Hopefully, the program won't have any more hiccups."

Everyone nodded in agreement. If Marjorie wouldn't open up to Emma, then they would get to Tiffany through Casey's connection to her. From here on, they would only meet if something big came up.

After everyone had filed out of his apartment, Andrew pulled out his phone and scrolled through his contacts, finally settling on one.

"It's me. We had the meeting like you suggested."

"And? Is everything safe?"

"So far, yes. We've mapped out a plan to talk to Ithaca's girlfriend."

"He had a girlfriend?"

"Turns out, yes."

"Now that you mention it, the track coaches said something about her yesterday. Well, keep me posted. I don't want this to cost you your scholarship."

"I said that we've got it under control. What are *you* doing?"

"I'm working on it, okay? I'm looking into it. *You* weren't able to get it back, so I have to find a work-around for it."

"*I wasn't able—*" Andrew sighed when he realized the call end had just ended. This had better be worth it.

Chapter 10

Whitham pulled out his phone and scrolled through his photos. He had snapped an image of the person leaving Delamont's house earlier that morning, but he didn't know who the man was. He had taken a photo of the person's car too. Squinting at the photo, he noticed a familiar sticker on the back windshield. Whoever it was, they were a staff member at Onore too. They had the staff parking lot decal to prove it.

He looked at the man's face again but still didn't recognize him. Luckily, the university kept an online photo directory of all program staff. It shouldn't take long to scroll through all of the images. Onore wasn't that large of a school. He opened the school's website on his home computer and navigated the links until he found the photo directory. He was surprised by the number of pages the directory housed. Maybe Onore was bigger than he thought. He started at the beginning of the alphabet and clicked through page after page of photos. More than once, he had to pause to compare his image to a staff photo, but none of the photos were of the guy he had spotted. He was starting to grow frustrated and realized that the car could have been the man's wife's vehicle. He'd never figure it out then! He had no choice but to keep clicking through the images. He was about to take a break and rest his eyes when the man's face emerged onto the screen. *Gotcha!* Closing his photo app, he mulled over the best course of action. How could he make contact with this guy?

* * * * * * * * *

Emma waited until she got home to call Marjorie. She thought about sending her a text but didn't know if she would be able to get much out of her over a text thread. She found her number from the group chat and hit talk.

"Hello? Is this Emma from the track team?"

"Yeah, hey, Marjorie. I just wanted to call and check in with you. How are you?"

"Oh, I'm...I'm hanging in there. It's been a hard twenty-four hours, I guess."

"I can't even imagine. I'm really sorry, Marjorie."

"Thanks, I appreciate it."

"Is there anything I can do for you?"

"Oh, no. I'm okay, really. Stephen's parents got here this morning, so I've been shuttling them around. It's been good to have that as a distraction. He was an only child, so they're basically in shock. We all are, I guess."

"Oh wow, I hadn't realized he was an only child. I guess I didn't really know him very well, to be honest. I'm sure it would be shocking to anyone. He seemed like he was in great shape. I guess you never know."

"He *was* in great shape. No one knows what happened. Even the medical examiner told Cort and Shirley, that's Stephen's parents, that he might not be able to figure it out without doing an autopsy. Cort and Shirley didn't want one, though. It won't bring him back, knowing what happened, right? So, they just want to move on from that and have their time to grieve."

Emma paused before speaking. She couldn't think of a way to ask if Marjorie knew about the powder without first telling her about the powder. "That's really hard. I keep saying that I'm sorry and I really am. If you need anything, please let me know. Even if it's just to talk."

"Thank you, Emma. My roommate has been really great. She is a good friend to have right now. I appreciate the phone call." She hung up.

Emma sighed. As much as she wanted to know if the program

was in further jeopardy, she couldn't grill this poor young woman when she was clearly suffering already. They would have to go to plan B. She sent a text to the group to report her failure.

* * * * * * * * * *

Andrew read Emma's text and thought about how best to respond. Casey only knew of Marjorie's roommate from the calculus class. They needed a better connection to get information from her. Casey responded before he could come up with an idea.

There's a review group that meets at the library on Sunday afternoons. She always goes. I could try to catch her afterwards?

Andrew still didn't think that was the right play. They needed someone that wasn't just a random acquaintance. He had an idea.

What if I go to the review session and ask her out on a date afterwards?

Jess and Casey didn't like that idea. Did he really think that any female on campus would swoon at the opportunity to date an athlete? Wiley stuck up for him, though. He told those girls that Andrew was pretty well known on campus. He held the homerun record and his face was on posters around not only the gym but other campus flyers. Casey remained firm, though.

Why don't you pretend to need extra help in calculus? You can borrow my book if you need to. She is really good at math. Always answers the questions in class. I don't even know why she goes to the review sessions. Ask her if she'll stay late and give you extra help.

Andrew mulled it over and thought it would work. He had already taken calculus in high school. He was a business major now, but he should be able to bluff his way through the review enough to look like he needed help.

* * * * * * * * * *

Derek read through the texts while lying in bed. He was
holding his phone in his left hand and tossing a football with his
right. All of this work to figure out what the girlfriend knew
seemed dumb to him if the program was still on hold. Did anyone
even know where the powder Dr. D was giving them had ended
up? He texted Alan.

You up

Yeah. Y

Is anyone taking over the program? I'm starting to get nervous about
it.

Me 2. No idea.

Should we talk to Whitham?

He creeps me out.

Same

But I'll call him tomorrow maybe.

K

Derek laid his phone on his chest and continued tossing the
football absentmindedly. It helped him focus. It seemed like
Whitham would want to keep the program going, so logically, the
only reason he wouldn't have contacted them about the next pick-
up would be that he didn't have the powder or didn't know where
it was.

* * * * * * * * * *

Marjorie laid back on her bed and pulled her comforter up
tightly under her chin. When she was little, she used to pull it all
the way up over her head if she got scared. The phone call from
Emma seemed thoughtful at first, but the more she went over the
conversation in her head, the more it bothered her. She had seen
Emma at the gym that morning in the media room. Someone from
campus police had been with them and two others that looked more
professionally dressed. *Detectives maybe?* She had gone up to the

gym to confront Dr. D, but then his office was sealed with crime scene tape. She hadn't been paying much attention to alerts from the school and realized that she had missed a couple. They had announced the death of Dr. John Delamont around eight that morning. *Murdered!* But the university wanted to assure everyone that the investigators felt it was an isolated event and that there was no reason to think the campus was unsafe.

But how could they know that? Marjorie shuddered. *His death had to be related to Stephen's, but how? And why? And why did Stephen's teammate call her?*

* * * * * * * * * *

Whitham went back to his office to access the school network. As the athletic director, he was able to view all of the schedules for the student athletes each semester. One by one, he pulled up the eight program members' schedules. One of them had to have a class with the guy he had photographed.

Finally, he found someone in one of the man's classes. This person could get into to the man's office through office hours. They could get the program back on track. Whitham knew the program was just as important to each of the athletes as it was to him. It wouldn't take much convincing to get them to snoop around some. He pulled up the photo again and found the share button. Scrolling through his contacts, he found the athlete's name and shared the photo.

I know you are in this man's class. He has the powder. Find a way to get it back.

His young friend responded.

What? Why does he have the powder? Why can't u get it?

Whitham responded.

I know that he has it. Find a way to get it back. Without the powder, you could lose everything. You know the man. I've never met him.

106

He waited for a response.
I can't exactly just ask for the powder, right?
He typed in a response.
Probably not. Figure out where he keeps it. Get it back.

Chapter 11

After Cari turned in her article, she drove back to her apartment to unwind before meeting Genevieve later. She wanted to try to get Marjorie on the phone again. She pulled up her number again and hit send.

"Hello?" Marjorie spoke in a tired voice.

"Marjorie. I'm sorry to bother you again."

"No, you're not. You're just trying to get a scoop. I don't know anything!" She cried.

Cari spoke quickly. "Please don't hang up. Please. I'm not in it for a scoop. It was awful what happened to Stephen. I'm trying to help."

"You can't help. Don't you see? I tried to go see Dr. Delamont this morning. I looked up his office number and walked over to the gym to see him, but the whole thing was cordoned off with crime scene tape. He was *murdered*!" Her voice trembled.

"Marjorie, please, please calm down." Cari heard someone else talking to her in the background.

"It's okay, Tiff. I'm fine." She said away from the phone, though Cari still heard it. "Sorry, Ms. Turnlyle. That was my roommate. She heard me getting upset and was worried."

"I heard about Dr. Delamont, but why were you going to see him?"

"Stephen mentioned him to me once. He was the one that Stephen went to for the nutritional program, but it wasn't really nutrition. Just a second."

Cari heard Marjorie walking and then a door closing and then some more walking.

"Stephen told me that he wasn't supposed to talk about it but this Dr. Delamont gave him some sort of special protein powder once a month. I didn't like it. It sounded like steroids to me, you know? But Stephen promised me that it wasn't. He said that it wasn't illegal; it just wasn't widely known. Dr. Delamont only gave it to a few of the athletes. It isn't a banned substance. But..."

"But you're worried that it somehow contributed to his death." Marjorie choked back a sob. "Yes, but you can't write about this! It would kill his parents. Stephen has always been a rule follower, a good kid, you know? He would never try to cheat or anything. He trusted this Delamont guy, but I don't. And now he's dead and I don't know what to think!"

"Don't worry, Marjorie, I would never publish something you weren't comfortable with. I'm here to help, not hurt. Why don't we meet somewhere? Maybe for coffee tomorrow or something?"

"I can't meet. Don't you see? Someone killed Delamont because of this powder. I'm certain of it. The police had this whole group of athletes at the gym yesterday. They were interviewing them in the big media room when I walked past, trying to find Delamont's office. One of them called me today! I don't want to get involved." She ended the call.

Cari gripped her phone tighter in frustration. She couldn't gain traction on this if she couldn't get anyone to talk to her. She knew there was a story here and she was determined to get to the bottom of it. Cari sighed. She still had an hour before meeting with Genevieve. She decided to take a shower. Maybe it would help her organize her thoughts. Marjorie had sounded really scared. *The phone call from the other athlete had really spooked her.*

Before she could get in the shower, her phone buzzed with another incoming call. It was her editor. She wondered what would drive him to call her on a Saturday evening. Her article had been completely fact-based; she didn't make any conjectures about Ithaca's death, calling it a tragedy and nothing more. She ran her thumb across the screen to take the call.

"Turnlyle speaking."

"Cari, what is this I hear about you trying to interview the track coach today?"

"Sir? I do cover the sports section."

"He called my office today to complain that both you and Cardian were harassing him and his assistant coaches."

"I spoke to him once in regards to the death at the track meet yesterday, sir. I was hoping to get a quote about the athlete, but he refused and directed me to the media relations person."

"Well, he got the impression that you were trying to dig up dirt on his athletes as well as that doctor who died. Delacrow? Dela-something."

"Mr. Ollaman, I promise you, I was not calling about Dr. Delamont. That's Lionel's story. I can't speak for what he did today."

Ollaman growled at her. "I can't have my reporters gallivanting around harassing the entire community every time something exciting happens. We need the community on our side or no one will talk to us. Did you call the media representative?"

"Again, sir. I did not overstep my bounds. When he told me no, I moved on. I didn't call the media relations person because I didn't need a generalized *no comment* statement from the university. I was hoping to write a nice article about the student who died, but the death of the sports medicine doctor seems to be overshadowing things."

"Well, she called me too. She said that my reporters needed to learn to use the proper channels when it came to speaking with people at her university. She had several calls from coaches complaining. Who else did you call?"

"I didn't call any other coaches, sir. I went to track practice to try to track down some of Ithaca's friends or his girlfriend, but I did not try to interview another coach."

"I do not want to hear about you trying to scoop Cardian. He's been with the Beagle longer than you've been alive. He might be a little rough around the edges, but he gets the story written. Stay in your lane, Turnlyle." He ended the call.

Cari looked at the ceiling in frustration. She didn't want to get on the wrong side of her boss. She wondered what made Cardian call the track coach too. Surely, he hadn't already realized that the two deaths were connected. *He probably called all of the head coaches to see what their interactions with Delamont had been like.* She nodded her head; Cardian didn't know anything. She picked up her notebook and made a note to look into some of the other athletic programs. Marjorie had mentioned there were several athletes that the police had interviewed that morning. There must be some other students that had worked closely with Delamont. She checked her watch. She still had time to shower before meeting Genevieve.

* * * * * * * * *

Genevieve arrived at O'Zook's a few minutes early. She wanted to get a seat in the back where she could see the door and the rest of the restaurant. It was really more of a bar than a restaurant, especially after eight o'clock. It looked like a bit of a dive from the outside, with one of the Os not being fully lit anymore and the apostrophe hanging a little crooked. The inside was kept clean and you couldn't find better chips and queso anywhere in the state. *And their margaritas weren't too bad either*, she thought. She considered ordering one for both Cari and herself and then wondered if she should bypass the alcohol since she was meeting Cari as part of the investigation. Still, Alex wasn't with her, so it wasn't an official interview. She signaled to the waitress that she was ready to place an order.

Cari walked in right as the waitress was bringing the drinks to the back booth. She was wearing a long beige cardigan over a lime green top, skinny jeans, and leather boots. It had been a few years since they had graduated from college, but Cari didn't look a day older or a pound heavier. Genevieve glanced down at her SUNY college sweatshirt, old jeans, and sneakers feeling a little underdressed. *Too late to worry about it now!* She waved Cari over to the booth.

Cari took her bag off of her shoulder and slid across from Genevieve. "Thanks for agreeing to meet me. I know it's kind of against policy."

Genevieve frowned. "I thought you were here to offer me information, not the other way around."

Cari flashed a smile. "Of course. I didn't mean to imply otherwise. It's so great to see you, Gen!"

Just then, Genevieve saw the waitress approaching with her chips and queso order. She flicked her head at Cari to indicate that she needed to zip it for a minute.

"Can I get you anything else? Did you need to see a menu?" The waitress asked.

"Actually, I would take a water and if I could get a cheeseburger all the way, that would be great." The waitress wrote her order down and waited for Genevieve to respond too.

Genevieve's eyes betrayed her surprise. "I didn't realize we were getting dinner here too. I guess I could go for a water too, thanks."

"Sorry. I know it's late, but I didn't have a chance to eat. I've been running all over the place all day and sometimes you can just go for a burger, you know?" She cringed inwardly, realizing she sounded just like all the students she'd been speaking with all day. "I'm starving."

Genevieve waited for the waitress to walk away before speaking again. "You mentioned in your text that you had some interesting information on Hartfeld?"

Cari took a breath. "Yes, I take it you've spoken to him already too?"

"Yes, he was our victim's emergency contact. No next of kin

was listed."

"Right. I read that Delamont's parents died a few years ago. Anyway, I found Hartfeld when I was searching for background info on Delamont. They were high school friends, apparently."

"And what or should I say, *who* led you to Delamont in the first place?" Genevieve questioned her.

Cari sealed her lips. "Come on now. I said that I'd share information, not give away my sources here, Gen. Should I continue?" She paused, waiting for Genevieve to concede. "Okay then. I found an article from a few years back when Delamont was hired. Turns out he's from here and moved back at the encouragement of his longtime friend, Dr. Bryan Hartfeld.

"Hartfeld is a bit of a shifty character, in my opinion. Again, I didn't want to reveal my source or my real reasons for speaking with him, so I spun him some yarn about doing an article on hometown kids returning to the nest. He was more than happy to tell me all about himself when he thought he was going to be in the newspaper.

"But his mood kept switching from proud scientist to angry old man. One minute, he'd be droning on about his hamsters, the next he'd be shaking his finger in my face in outrage."

"What would make him so angry?"

Before Cari could answer, the waitress returned with their food and two waters. Cari thanked her and then immediately tore into her cheeseburger before answering the question. Genevieve snacked on a few chips while waiting for Cari to speak again.

"He started to tell me about some of his research with the hamsters. He showed me how some of them could run faster because he had found a way to supplement their nutrition through an additive he developed in his lab. I said it sounded like hamster steroids and he did *not* like that. It was like he came unhinged. It happened again when I asked if it had been tested in people."

Genevieve thought for a moment. "I don't see how this ties into

113

Delamont at all, though."

"Here's the thing. I can't tell you how I got tipped off to looking at Delamont, but you know that I cover the sports section. I was looking into the death of the student athlete at the track meet yesterday and my research led me to Delamont. The deaths are related somehow and I think it has to do with this guy's research." She took another large bite.

"It's a lot of conjecture, though, Cari. It's circumstantial. The ME told us that the kid's death was from natural causes. Coincidences *do* happen, despite what you read in crime novels."

Cari's shoulders slumped. "Surely, you aren't going to dismiss my theory so easily?"

"What do you want me to do? Accuse the mad scientist of poisoning hamsters?" She tilted her head at Cari. "I agree, Dr. Hartfeld is not normal, but being abnormal doesn't make you guilty of something."

"I thought we could work together on this, Gen. You're not even trying to meet me halfway."

"Cari, you haven't given me any reason, any evidence that ties these two deaths together. I know you don't want to compromise your sources, but if all you have is that our victim has a friend that does research on hamsters, then I think you have nothing." She looked at her friend sympathetically. Genevieve could see that Cari was struggling to maintain her composure, but there was something else.

"You're holding something back. I can't work with you on this if I don't have all the facts. What are you not telling me?" Genevieve asked.

Cari took a breath. "There's…" She looked away for a moment before meeting Genevieve's eyes again. "There's nothing else. I have to go." She pulled some cash from her purse and laid it on the table before walking away.

Genevieve sighed. She couldn't share details of an open

investigation with a reporter. She was intrigued by Cari's meeting with Dr. Hartfeld, though. Something about the man didn't sit right with her, but she wasn't sure if it was his goofy mannerisms or that he'd lied to them about how recently he'd spoken with Delamont.

She had promised Alex that she would update him with whatever Cari shared with her. She didn't want to talk about it anymore in the restaurant though, so she signaled the waitress for the bill. Cari had barely touched the margarita. Genevieve felt bad about how things had ended with her. She was still new to being a detective and didn't want to compromise her job by possibly leaking details of her case to the media. She and Cari had been good friends in high school, but could she still trust her now? When the waitress returned, Genevieve double checked the charges and then added some of her own cash to what Cari had left. Then she slid out of the booth and towards the exit. It was time to give Alex a call.

* * * * * * * * * *

Cari slammed the door to her Toyota Camry and thrust her key into the ignition. She felt like a fool for thinking that Genevieve would want to work together on the investigation. She had come this close to revealing what Marjorie had told her about the powder. To be fair, Ben had told her about it too, but he hadn't known that it came from Delamont. Marjorie had shared that with her and Marjorie was scared. Cari didn't want to jeopardize the young woman's trust and lose her as a source altogether. How could she get Genevieve to believe that the deaths were connected without talking about the powder?

She started the car and pointed it in the direction of her apartment. Even though she felt too keyed up to sleep, she didn't know where else to go right now. She was running out of leads to chase and needed to regroup.

* * * * * * * * * *

"Runimoss. Go."

"Alex. You know it's me." Genevieve rolled her eyes as she buckled her seatbelt. She had gotten a good deal on the 2017 Ford Expedition. It was kind of a large vehicle for a single woman, but she liked being able to see around people in front of her. Plus, it was the same make and model as her car in high school, so she was used to how it handled.

"How did it go with your reporter friend?"

"It was kind of a bust. I think she wanted to tell me more, but was hesitant to compromise her source. She thinks the deaths of the student athlete and Delamont are connected."

"Why?"

Genevieve could hear the doubt in her partner's voice. "She met with Dr. Hartfeld today—"

"The scientist guy? How did she find out about him?"

"She wouldn't say, except that when she started looking into the athlete's death, she stumbled onto Delamont, which led her to his friend, Hartfeld."

"How did she find out about Delamont? I know his death isn't a secret, but still."

"Again, she wouldn't say, but her meeting with Hartfeld was a little weird. She said that he would go from really angry to really chill in just a moment depending on what questions she asked."

"The guy's a weirdo, so what?"

"That was what I said, but she thinks his research with hamsters ties into this somehow."

"Hamsters?! Hamsters? Are you for real, Gen?"

Genevieve fought the impulse to laugh with her desire to defend Cari. "I don't really understand it either, Alex. There's something else that she wasn't telling me; maybe that ties it

116

together more."

"Well, I got the financial records for both Hartfeld and Whitham while you were at the bar." He paused and she could hear him flipping through some papers. "Hartfeld has almost zero living expenses. I think his parents possibly still own that house. He doesn't pay rent or a mortgage. He's got basic bills that he pays on time every month. It looks like he might use some of his salary to pay for some of his lab stuff, which seems weird, but I'm not really familiar with that arena. Maybe people do it all the time.

"Anyway, Whitham's a completely different story. Guy has a huge mortgage that he can barely cover. He bought a Jag recently that is way out of his budget too. He's racking up credit card debt left and right."

"Money trouble is obviously a common motive, but I don't see how it fits here. What does Whitham gain by Delamont's death? Whitham was the boss, not the other way around."

"True. It's still worth looking into. The murder doesn't look pre-meditated, more of a heat of the moment kind of thing. And money trouble can cause stress."

"Both of them are hiding something. We need to dig a little deeper into their backgrounds."

"Well, we've already agreed that we found Hartfeld to be suspicious. We know he lied about when he last spoke with Delamont. I'm still not sure that this is enough to bring him into the station. What do you think?"

"I know earlier today I wanted to bring him in, but now I kind of want to see if we can meet him at his lab. Maybe we can find out some more about whatever is bothering Cari with these hamsters."

"It's too late to call him now. We'll have to catch him in the morning. I'll get it set up. 8:30 tomorrow?"

"Works for me. I'll meet you at the station so we can ride there together." She ended the call.

Chapter 12

Marjorie was running down a hallway. She quickly glanced over her shoulder and saw that they were gaining on her. She put her head down and tried to pick up speed even though her lungs were burning. Legs screaming, she saw Stephen exit the hallway through the double doors up ahead. If she could just reach him, she knew she'd be safe. She could hear their footsteps getting closer. How were they so fast? The hallway seemed to grow in length as she pushed herself to reach the doors. Just as she pushed the door open, it disappeared. Someone shoved her from behind and she was falling, falling...she screamed—

"Marjorie! Marjorie! Wake up. It's okay. It's just a dream." Tiff was next to her, gently shaking her shoulder.

Marjorie rubbed her eyes and looked around the room. The dream had seemed so real. Stephen had seemed so real. She looked up at Tiff, who had a towel wrapped around her head. She was wearing a bathrobe and her feet were bare. "What time is it?"

"It's only 7:30. I had just gotten out of the shower when I heard you screaming. You really scared me at first. I'm glad it was just a dream. Are you okay now?"

"Yeah, I'm okay. Just a bad dream." She touched her head, trying to calm herself. Her heart was still racing as though she had actually been running. "Is it Sunday?"

"Yes, Sunday morning. My co-worker asked if I could open the ice cream shop for her today at nine. I'm not on shift until the evening though. I can tell her no if you need me to stay."

"No, don't turn that down for me. I'm picking Stephen's parents up for brunch later. They were upset yesterday because the ME wouldn't release his body to them yet. They just want to go home, you know? I feel so bad for them."

Leslie A. Piggott

"Why won't they release his body?"

"I'm not totally sure. Shirley and Cort said something about a complication." She yawned and shrugged. "I think they were going to call over there again today. It will work out."

Tiffany nodded. "I'm planning on leading my study group this afternoon at the library still. I'll have my phone with me. If you need anything, you know how to reach me."

"Thank you, but really, I'm fine. I'm coping. Helping Stephen's parents is helping me get through this. It's good. I'm good." She bobbed her head up and down, trying to convince herself as much as Tiff.

"Okay, but don't feel like you need to soldier on. It's okay to ask for help sometimes." Tiff smiled. "I'm going to go finish getting ready. I'll probably grab lunch at the student center before my group starts."

She turned and left the room, closing the door behind her. Marjorie sighed. Maybe she should find someone to talk to about Stephen or about her dream. She shuddered, remembering the faces of the people chasing her. Each of them angry and shouting her name as they raced after her. Eight faces. Seven of which she had only seen once before.

* * * * * * * * *

Cari got up early to run a few miles before sitting down to organize her notes again. As she was running, she heard her mom's voice in the back of her mind, *Are you going to church today, sweetie?* Cari lowered her eyes. She had kind of let her church attendance slide since Christmas, well maybe it was Easter last year. It seemed like she was always chasing a new story and finding an excuse not to be there. It's not that it wasn't important to her; she was just really career driven and needed to prove herself. That meant going the extra mile sometimes and making some personal sacrifices.

119

Once things settled down, she would start up the habit again.

As she pounded down the trail near her apartment, she mentally went through her checklist for the day. She needed to call Bob again and see if he had an update for her. She needed to talk to Marjorie but didn't know how to approach her. She didn't know where she lived or how to find her. *I just need to be gently persuasive. She'll come around.*

She wanted to look into Hartfeld some more. He had really rubbed her the wrong way. One moment he seemed like an eccentric, absent-minded-professor. The next, he was angry and accusatory, even threatening in his tone. He was hiding something behind that anger, but what?

Cari finished her five-mile loop and climbed the steps up to her apartment. She had left her phone on *do not disturb* while she was running to help herself stay focused. She fished her phone out of her running belt with one hand and her apartment key with the other. She had a missed call and two texts from her mom. She sighed as she unlocked her door. Making her mother wait never made the conversation easier, but she also wanted to talk to Bob. She texted him asking if he felt like coffee—her treat! She refilled her water bottle and then sat down to call her mom back. Putting the phone on speaker, she opened her messaging app in case Bob wrote back quickly.

"Cari!" Her mom's voice rang through the small apartment. "Good morning, sunshine! I hope I didn't wake you up with my call."

Cari rolled her eyes, knowing that her mom hoped the exact opposite. "No, you didn't. I was out running."

"Now, Cari. Did you run with a group? Did you at least bring the mace we got you for Christmas?"

"Mom. I'm almost thirty years old. I'm careful. Please don't worry."

"When you have children of your own, you'll understand how

futile it is to tell a mother not to worry." She paused. *Here it comes,* Cari thought, *she's going to ask about church.*

"How is your friend, um, what's his name? Um, Bob? What is he up to?"

Cari should have known she would go this route first. "Bob seems fine. I talked to him yesterday morning, in fact."

"Oh, how nice. He always seemed like such a nice young man. How opportune it was that you both got jobs in the same city! Like fate, huh?"

Cari groaned. "Mom, I've told you. Bob is just a friend."

"Well, I'm just saying. You have to be friends first, you know. Doesn't he go to your church too?"

And there it was. The real reason she had called. "I see him at church sometimes too, Mom."

"Maybe you'll see him there this morning! You *are* going this morning?" It sounded like more of a declaration than a question.

"Mom, I—"

"Cari! You haven't been in weeks. This isn't like you."

"Mom, I don't want to argue about it. I will make it a priority next week, okay? I promise. I really have to go. I love you." She ended the call before her mom could protest again.

Thankfully, Bob had time for coffee and suggested that they meet at nine at the shop down the street from her place. She realized that she didn't actually know where Bob lived even though they had both been in the city for a few years. She shrugged. *Bob was a pretty private person. If he wanted me to know where he lived, then I'd know.*

She finished her water while she threw together a fruit smoothie for breakfast. She'd grab a bagel at the coffee shop later. She had just enough time to jump in the shower before meeting Bob.

* * * * * * * * * *

121

Dr. Hartfeld rummaged around his kitchen for something to eat. He had run out of cereal again and forgotten to buy more. He wasn't a coffee drinker; it made him too jittery. He looked in his pantry again for something that could pass for breakfast. He really needed to go to the grocery store more regularly. Reaching to the back of the top shelf, his fingers curled around a plastic wrapper of some sort. *Please don't be moldy, please don't be moldy.* He pulled the package down and discovered a sleeve of peanut butter crackers. *These never go bad.* He smiled and tore into the package. He made a mental note to stop by the store on his way home from the lab.

Sitting down at his table, his phone chirped that he had received a text message. He unlocked it and opened his messaging app. The message was from an unknown sender. Whoever sent it had somehow hidden their number too.

I know what you did

A chill ran up his spine.

Who is this? He responded.

Someone who can help you if you help me

What was this person talking about? He didn't need any help. Help with what?

What are you talking about?

We both know what I'm talking about. Give me what you know I want and no one else has to know.

Go to hell. You don't know anything.

Hartfeld threw his phone at the sofa across the room from him. Who would threaten him? What did they think they knew? The phone hit the sofa and immediately started ringing. He glared at it and refused to answer. Now this person was calling him?! *I don't think so, Jack.* He let it go to voice mail and went back to eating his crackers. He had barely finished one when the phone rang again. Growling, he got up to see who it was.

The screen was flashing with an actual phone number instead of *Unknown number* like the messages had shown. It was a local number, but he still didn't answer it. The phone beeped, indicating that he had received a voice mail. He started to pull it up when the phone started ringing again. It was the same number. He was really tempted to answer it, but also afraid of who might be on the line. He silenced the call and went back to the voice mail.

Dr. Hartfeld. It's Detective Runimoss. We came across a few things during our investigation yesterday that we wanted to ask you about. Please give me a call back when you get this.

He pulled his wallet out of his pocket and flipped through the various pockets for the female detective's card. He would rather talk to her than the man-giant that was her partner. Where had he put that? He patted his hands on the front of his pants to see if he'd stuck it in there, but the pockets were empty. *Oh well. If they really want to talk to me, they will just have to find me.*

* * * * * * * * * *

Genevieve pulled up to the station to meet Alex. She hadn't heard from him yet, but maybe he was still making arrangements to meet Hartfeld. She debated about waiting outside for him to join her or going inside. Someone had probably already made coffee inside and even though it would be terrible, it was still better than no coffee, which was her current alternative. She pocketed her keys after locking the car and walked inside to find Alex.

After pouring herself a cup from the station's Mr. Coffee maker, she walked back to her and Alex's desks. He looked grumpy already, which was not a good sign. He waved her over.

"Hartfeld didn't answer when I called. I left him a voicemail, but he hasn't called back."

"Maybe he was talking to somebody else and just hasn't gotten back to you yet."

"I called three times."

"Okay, so he knows we really want to talk to him. Do you want to just go pick him up? I thought you didn't think we had enough on him to bring him in."

Alex groaned. "We don't. Let's call CSU and see if they can find anything else for us. I know the vic's car was a dead end—they only found his prints in it, but maybe there's something else on his phone."

Genevieve picked up her desk phone and pressed the extension for CSU.

"CSU, Chris speaking."

"Hey, Chris, it's Detective Viacorte. I'm calling about the Delamont case. The vic's phone, can you look through it again?"

"What am I looking for exactly?"

"I'm not really sure. Is there a way to find deleted files or something? We've kind of hit a brick wall in the investigation and we need to stir up some new leads."

"I'll search the cache and see if there's anything hiding on the SIM card. That messaging app might have a web version too. If so, sometimes we can pull up a history that isn't available on the mobile version. I'll keep you posted."

"Thanks, Chris. I appreciate it."

She put the receiver back in the cradle and turned to Alex. "They're going to check into a few things, see what shakes out."

"We're operating under the impression that he was meeting someone at his office yesterday morning. Whoever he met was most likely the last person to see him alive and also most likely our killer. There has to be a record of the meeting, right?"

"It seems logical, but having never used that app, I can't say for sure. Maybe it's like Snapchat where it deletes the message immediately after it's seen."

"That seems like a stupid feature." He rolled his eyes.

"Well, while we wait to hear back from CSU, why don't we go

over our notes again. Maybe we missed something."

"Maybe Hartfeld will call back. Maybe I'll win a million dollars and I can retire." Alex threw his hands up over his head in frustration.

"Don't be such a grump, Alex. We're still moving on this." She tried to sound more hopeful than she felt.

* * * * * * * * * *

Andrew woke with a start. It was Sunday. Why was his alarm ringing? He didn't need to get up early today. It was a rest day. He could see the sunlight peeking through the edge of the blinds in his bedroom when he opened his eyes. He had pressed the button on his alarm clock several times, but it wouldn't stop ringing. He looked over and saw the screen on his phone was lit up. Of course, his alarm clock didn't even ring! It played the local radio station. He grabbed the phone and swiped across the screen to answer it.

"It's Andrew."

"What's the status of the girl?" The familiar, gravelly voice asked him.

"We haven't really gotten to talk to her yet. She kind of gave us the slip yesterday."

"You don't have time for mistakes. If the wrong person finds out about the powder, it's gone along with your scholarship."

"It's gone? What do you mean, it's gone? It's already gone, man. Or did you get it back?"

"I told you. I'm working on it. You take care of your part and I'll take care of mine." The call ended.

Andrew groaned. He hated being this guy's lackey, but what choice did he have? He couldn't lose his scholarship, and without the powder, he'd never be able to keep it. Even worse, he'd never even be considered for the pros, not even Minor League. He had a few hours before he needed to leave for the study group. He decided not to worry about borrowing Casey's textbook. Most students used digital copies of books anymore, but he didn't want to purchase one of those either. He knew the library would have multiple copies, even if they were older editions. It would be good enough. He went into his bedroom to check his closet. Even if the girls thought asking the roommate out was doomed to fail, he still wanted to look good. You could never be too sure.

* * * * * * * * * *

Cari sat across from Bob at the coffee shop. Her hair was still wet from the shower, but she'd pulled it into a ponytail to keep it from getting her shirt wet too. It was Sunday, so she'd thrown on an old college t-shirt and jeans along with her sneakers. Bob was dressed in his usual attire of light khaki pants, a button-up shirt with a collar, and leather loafers. Most people didn't know, but he had naturally curly hair. He didn't like it, so he got frequent haircuts to keep the unruly curls at bay. Bob removed his beanie and smoothed his hair back into place. His friendly blue eyes sparkled as he looked at Cari.

"Are you sure you don't want something to eat? A bagel even?" She asked Bob.

"I had cereal before I left. Thanks anyway."

Cari took a bite of the coffee cake she had ordered before asking Bob about the case. She tried to compose her thoughts while she chewed.

"Did the ME release Ithaca's body yet?"

"No. He still has a hold on it. The parents aren't happy about it."

"Why is there a hold? Is it because of Delamont?"

Bob's eyes got big and he looked around the room carefully. "Cari! You're not supposed to know about him."

"Relax, the whole newsroom knows. No, I didn't tell them. It's been twenty-four hours now, Bob. It's old news."

"Okay, fine. But I don't know if that's why they won't release the other body. The ME didn't say."

"It seems probable, though, right? Two deaths on the same campus in less than twenty-four hours? What are the odds? Have you had to run any more tests related to Ithaca?"

"Cari, I'm not really supposed to talk about open cases."

Cari suppressed a sigh. "I'm not going to report it, Bob. We're friends. This is off-the-record."

"It feels like an interview, Cari."

"I'm sorry, Bob. It was really upsetting to see that kid go down. What if this happens to someone else? I couldn't live with myself if I ignored my gut feeling on this."

"Your gut feeling?"

"That the kid was taking something. Something made him collapse."

"I understand that you're upset, but even if I could tell you about the case, I don't have anything to tell. All I know is that they are holding his body."

"What about Delamont, then? I'm certain the deaths are related, and it sounds like someone at your station agrees with me. Who are they looking at for Delamont's murder?"

Bob sighed. "Off the record?"

Cari nodded. "Off the record, my friend." She slipped her hand into her pocket and hit a button on her recorder without Bob noticing.

* * * * * * * * *

Whitham paced in his office. He wished he could speed up time or peer into the future and see that everything was okay again. He reminded himself that it had only been less than two days, so there was no reason to panic. Yet. Still, it felt like his life was dangling from that proverbial precipice and it was going to fall the wrong way unless he did the right thing first.

He picked up his phone and dialed a number that was becoming increasingly familiar. No one answered and the person's voicemail soon played into his ear. Whitham debated ending the call without leaving a message but decided the person still needed a gentle shove in the right direction.

I need an update from you. Have you made contact with our guy? Call me and let me know. Sooner rather than later. I hope I don't have to remind you that several scholarships, including yours, depend on you making this happen. Be the team player that I know you are.

He hung up before the recording could cut him off. He didn't like being in the dark. Maybe he should take a more active role in the recovery process. He was about to set his phone down again when a text flashed on the screen.

Set up a meeting with him for help in his biochemistry class. I'll update after.

A meeting? Not good enough.

I could ask about working in his lab. It's something he offers for XC.

Cross Country?

Extra Credit

Oh. How soon would you start?

Idk. Gotta talk to him first.

Whitham drummed his fingers on the desk. He still wasn't convinced that this person was capable of getting anything from the professor. It was critical that they get the powder back. Maybe he could find a way to be more persuasive.

* * * * * * * * *

Marjorie sat down on her bed and stared off into space. She'd just dropped Stephen's parents off at their hotel again after eating brunch at a local café. She wondered if his parents felt as detached from reality as she did right now.

The ME had still refused to release his body to his parents. Stephen's mom had wept as his dad begged, but no amount of pleading would change the decision. The ME said that someone further up the food chain had demanded that the body not be released to the family yet. Marjorie hadn't mentioned the death of the sports medicine doctor to Shirley and Cort. She felt guilty somehow about it. If she'd pressed Stephen about that powder more, maybe he wouldn't have taken it. Maybe he'd still be alive.

She shook her head. She knew his death wasn't her fault. In fact, no one had even said that his death was suspicious or anything. They had said *natural causes*, but still, she wondered. Stephen had been an athlete for as long as she had known him. He'd never been sick or suffered from any sort of chronic illness. *What was in that powder?* The more she thought about it, the more certain she felt that it was at the center of this entire disaster. Maybe she should call that reporter back, but she was afraid that the woman just wanted to sensationalize Stephen's death. Marjorie didn't want to tarnish his image. He didn't deserve that.

Chapter 13

Genevieve looked through her notes for what must have been the tenth time that morning. Whitham had motive to kill Delamont; he was drowning in debt. Money was always a good motive, but she wasn't sure how it fit in with Delamont's death. She thought back to her conversation with Cari.

Cari had reason to believe that something with Hartfeld tied Delamont's death to the track star's collapse and death. She said that he did research on hamsters, which seemed completely meaningless to Genevieve. Her friend had been so adamant that Genevieve felt obligated to dig into Hartfeld a little more. He still hadn't returned Alex's call, but that didn't mean she couldn't use the internet to get more information. She opened a browser window and typed his name into the search bar along with 'hamsters' even though that seemed ridiculous. The search returned zero results. Genevieve sighed. She deleted hamsters and added the name of the university to the search. His lab webpage was the first result on the list. She clicked on the link.

Hartfeld was a member of the biochemistry department, which she already knew. He also lectured in undergraduate classes, as Tommy had told them. She clicked on the *Research Topics* tab. The page listed several papers that Hartfeld's lab had authored, but the titles were meaningless to Genevieve. She had taken biology and chemistry in high school, but that was it. She scrolled down the list of articles, pausing when she saw the word *metabolism*. Maybe this was what Cari was keying in on; Hartfeld researched metabolism. How did that tie into Delamont though? She looked over at Alex, who was angrily sorting the paperwork on his desk.

"Alex, did you take biology or chemistry in college?"

"Did I what? Why would I take those classes?"

"I took them in high school, but for my criminology degree, I focused more on psychology than biology. There were two different tracks. I didn't want to be a lab rat, so I went the other direction."

Alex raised his eyebrows as if to say, *great, who cares?*

"Anyway, Hartfeld does research on metabolism. I think that maybe Cari thinks that's what ties all of this together, but why? I thought if you understood some of this science stuff, maybe we could put two and two together here."

"Still with the reporter? You know she was just fishing for inside information. I'm a zero on science, Gen. Sorry."

"Metabolism, though. That's like nutrition, right?"

"Oh, I see what you're getting at. Yeah, I think those are related. I still feel like we're missing something. None of the athletes said anything about Dr. Hartfeld. I don't think they even know who he is."

Genevieve shrugged. "I didn't specifically ask them. At that point, he was just the emergency contact."

"If he doesn't call back soon, then let's just go to his house again. He can't hide from us forever."

Before she could agree, her desk phone rang with a call from CSU. She grabbed it.

"Chris! Tell me you've got something for us."

"Maybe, maybe not. I wasn't able to find any history in the cache or the SIM card, but the app did have a web version!"

"And?" Genevieve asked excitedly.

"He had a deleted meeting request for yesterday morning at 6:45. It didn't show up in the app anymore because the person who requested it also canceled it."

"I'm on the edge of my seat here, Chris. Who? Who had requested a meeting?"

"It only gave me an account number, so I had to request the identity of the user from the app developer."

Genevieve's heart sank. "And they wouldn't release it without a warrant."

"Exactly, but!"

"But what?"

"There was also a phone number associated with the meeting request. I put in a request for the owner of the number. Unless it's unlisted, we should get that back soon."

"What's the number, Chris? We have a whole list of numbers and names that were contacts for Delamont that the school gave us."

"Awesome. Let me find it in my notes here, just a sec."

She waited while he shuffled papers around and then came back on the line to read the number to her. She was ready with a pencil to record the new one. She repeated the number back to him to make sure that she hadn't transposed any of the digits.

"This is a big help, Chris. Thanks so much! Gotta run." She hung up.

"Do you have that list of phone numbers and names handy, Alex?"

He rifled through the paperwork on his desk again until he found the page she was asking for. "I got it right here. What's the number?"

"817-634-9989."

"That number belongs to one Andrew Niles. We could probably get a warrant to search his home."

"Let's put in a request, but I also want to bring him in. I'm going to call Chris back and see if they can triangulate his location. Who knows where he is on a Sunday?"

* * * * * * * * * *

Genevieve and Alex went down to the CSU lab to see if Chris could locate the whereabouts of Andrew Niles' phone. The athlete hadn't mentioned scheduling a meeting with Delamont that morning. The fact that he'd deleted the meeting request was very suspicious.

Alex held the door for Genevieve when they reached the CSU. She stepped into the lab space and walked over to Chris' desk.

"How did you get stuck working on a Sunday?" She asked him.

"We all get assigned shifts. It's my turn for the full weekend haul." He motioned to his computer screen. "I pulled up the number you want to triangulate. Unfortunately, the user doesn't have his phone on right now, so we can't ping its location."

"Can we get a back log or history of his previous locations?" Alex asked.

"Not without a warrant. The cell phone companies have pretty strict privacy policies."

Genevieve pursed her lips. "Well, he's not going to leave his phone off forever. No teenager could handle that. Can you keep this search active for us and let us know when the phone does turn on?"

"That I can do." Chris nodded.

"Thanks, man. We appreciate it." Alex turned back towards the exit. "Why don't we try to track Hartfeld down while we're waiting to hear back from Chris on this kid's phone?"

"He seems like the type to only be at his lab or his house, so where do we want to check first?"

Chris interrupted them. "Does this Hartfeld guy have a cell? I can add him to the search if you have his number."

The detectives turned around. "Of course, that would be *so* much easier than driving around town to find him."

Genevieve opened the case file and found Hartfeld's cell phone number. She read it off to Chris and verified that he had entered it correctly into his search program. The application gave the same result as before, *no signal found.*

"Are you sure this thing is accurate? Like its server isn't down or something?" Alex asked Chris.

Chris rolled his eyes. "I'm sure and I'll prove it to you. Let's check your phone then, Detective. What's the number?"

Alex entered his number with the keypad. Almost immediately, the address of the precinct popped up on the screen. He shrugged.

"You never know with technology." He frowned. "Let's keep the search active for both of these numbers. NOT for my number."

Chris grinned. "Aye, aye, Captain."

Genevieve followed Alex back to the elevator. It felt like they were continually running into a brick wall. With every good lead, they were hit with an obstacle that prevented them from moving forward.

* * * * * * * * * *

Cari returned to her office after meeting with Bob. Her friend had told her that the detectives were looking closely at both Bryan Hartfeld and Curtis Whitham. He didn't know the names of the athletes they had interviewed on campus yesterday, but he did know that there were eight of them. They had selected the eight because of an app Delamont used on his cell phone. As she walked into the newsroom, she saw Cardian walking past her desk with a cup of coffee. He looked her way when he heard the door open.

"Working on a weekend? What are you chasing, Miss Turnlyle?" The large man asked her. He was balding noticeably but wore a toupee that did a terrible job of hiding it. The man had to be at least seventy years old and had a gut that got larger every year. He was vain, arrogant, and everything that was irritating about old men. He had a southern drawl that was distinctive. She wondered if he was actually from the south or if he added the accent to make himself have more charisma somehow. Everything about him seemed fake.

"Good morning, Lionel. I'm just here to work on a follow up story from the track meet last week." She eyed him cautiously. Rumors still floated around the office that Cardian was a bit of a womanizer and had dodged a few sexual harassment cases over the years.

"A follow up story on a track meet? Could there be anything more boring? Who wants to read about the track meet in the first place?"

Cari forced her lips into a smile. "I think a lot of our athletes like to see their names in print, if nothing else."

"Say, I've been meaning to ask you. I was trying to get some interviews with some of the athletic coaches over at the university, but they all froze me out. Pissants. You do sports. Help me get some interviews with these people and it could be beneficial to you in the long run."

She turned her head sideways. "Beneficial how?"

"I'd put in a good word for you with our dear ole editor here. Get you moved out of sports faster." He winked.

Cari fought back a gag. "I would *love* to help you out, Lionel, but our editor told me not to bother any of the coaches this weekend. He's been taking some heat from it. The media relations person chewed him out already once."

"That media relations girl is no help at all! She just gave me the form statement that they issued to all the news outlets. I need an interview, damnit!" He shook his fist in the air.

"I'm afraid that you're asking the wrong person. That's above my pay grade." She shrugged and walked around him to her desk. "Good luck with your story, Lionel." She said dismissively as she sat down at her desk. He scowled at her and walked away. Served him right, the old goat. He was so far behind on this story and he didn't even know it.

* * * * * * * * *

135

Andrew strolled into the library conference room for the calculus review session. Casey had described Tiffany as a curvy blonde with glasses. He glanced around the room. There were already six people sitting at the table with their notebooks out and their books open. He was glad that he'd come early and checked out one of the library's copies of the book. He knew right away which student was Tiffany. She was the only one wearing glasses. Mentally, he chastised Casey for describing the girl as curvy. *More like overweight plus*, he thought. He took his backpack off of his shoulder and walked over to the side of the table where Tiffany was sitting.

"Are you Tiffany?" He asked quietly.

"That's me." She smiled and nodded.

"A friend of mine said that there was a calculus review session here right now. Is that what this is?"

"You've come to the right place, sir. What's your name?"

"Andrew Niles. I've gotten a little behind in class because of baseball and need to get back on track."

"I'm sure we can get you caught up. We were just about to start. Why don't you have a seat?"

Tiffany got up and went to the whiteboard. She instructed the other students that she would be starting with the chapter review work on page 247. Andrew quickly flipped to the page. He vaguely recognized the graphs and symbols from high school. Hopefully, enough of it would come back to him that he could ask some coherent questions and not blow his cover. *It sure would be easier to just ask this girl on a date.*

The review session seemed to drag on forever. Andrew tried to casually check his watch without looking bored. They had finally made it to the last problem in the review set. Tiffany put the marker down after writing the problem on the whiteboard.

"Andrew, would you like to walk us through this one?"

He tried not to show his shock. He had been writing all of the answers into his notebook like everyone else, but he had not recognized how they were solving any of them. He stood up slowly.

"Uh, sure, but I'll probably need a little coaching with it." He grinned at Tiffany.

"We're right behind you, Andrew. Literally. We'll be right here." She giggled at her joke.

He hoped his smile didn't look as fake as it felt. He walked over to the whiteboard and picked up the marker.

"Okay, so to solve this last one, the first thing you need to do is..." he stalled.

"Integrate within the limits..." Tiffany started, raising her eyebrows in an encouraging manner.

Integrate, limits. The terms were still just familiar to him. He looked at the symbols on the board and felt his frustration growing. Tiffany spoke up again.

"Did you need your notebook?" She had picked it up off of the table and was walking it over to him.

"Oh, right. Thanks." He looked at the problems, but wasn't sure what any meant. "To integrate, we need to—"

"Good grief. We've done this like twenty-eight times already. Give me the marker." A short guy with acne and greasy hair walked up to the board and took the marker from Andrew. He stepped back, a little stunned.

"Theo, that was rude." Tiffany admonished him.

"Whatever. He obviously hasn't learned anything today or any other day." He quickly wrote the answer on the board and then sat back down.

Andrew shrugged sheepishly. "I guess I need a little more help if you have time."

"I'd be happy to stick around, Andrew. Everyone else, unless you have further questions, this is the end of our study session for today. We'll meet again next week. Same time, same place."

The other five students packed up their belongings and filed out of the room. Andrew sat down in front of his notebook again as Tiffany erased and cleaned the board.

"I really appreciate this. How long have you been leading this study group?"

"All semester. I really love math and I want to be a math professor one day. I'm hoping this will give me some experience."

"That's great. I do not love math, and I hope to not take another class again." He grinned at her in a teasing manner.

She laughed. "Well, maybe I can change your mind about that. Which section are you in?"

"Of the book? Or?" He was confused.

"No, silly. Which class? Who is your professor?"

"Oh, right. Sorry." He racked his brain trying to remember a math professor's name. "I should know that, but I've missed a few classes this semester and…" He should have asked Casey who the professor was. He was feeling more and more like an idiot with each passing second.

"I understand. Okay, it seems like integrals are really tripping you up. We've already done all the review questions, so why don't we go back a few sections and do some of the problems earlier in the chapter?"

"Works for me." He nodded.

They continued through the chapter for another hour. Andrew did his best to stay engaged and constantly complimented her teaching. While he had no desire to learn calculus again, he had to hand it to her. She was really good at explaining the material.

"I think I'm starting to get the hang of this. We have an exam next Thursday. I really need to do well on it, or I might get put on academic probation. Coach was pretty peeved at me for signing up for this class in the first place."

"You said that you're a business major. Why are you taking

138

calculus?"

Andrew had assumed this question would come up and had planned an answer for it. He made himself blush. "Would you believe it was for a girl?"

"What? You are taking calculus to impress a girl?"

"Not exactly. I was sort of dating a girl last semester and she was signing up for calculus. She thought it would be fun if we could take a class together. It seemed like a good idea at the time, but we didn't get into the same class. I only take twelve hours a semester so that I can focus mostly on baseball, so I had to stick with it even though it's not a credit that I need."

"She must be a pretty special girl to get you to take calculus," Tiffany said quietly.

"Actually, she broke up with me right after the semester started. She said that I was too into myself and baseball. Now I'm stuck taking calculus for no reason and looking like a fool."

"You are not a fool, Andrew. You made a lot of progress this afternoon."

"I had a great teacher." He smiled at her. "I really can't thank you enough for spending an extra hour with me. Can I take you to dinner or something? I owe you one."

"Oh, you don't need to do that. I'm happy to help."

"No, I insist. What kind of food do you like? Tex-Mex, Italian, Greek?"

"Well, Tex-Mex is my favorite, but really, you don't need to buy me dinner. Besides, I work at the ice cream parlor and my shift starts at 6. We'd have to go eat at 4:30 or something ridiculous." She giggled nervously.

"4:30 it is. I know a really great Tex-Mex place just off campus. I'll pick you up at 4:15?"

"Are you sure? Wow. Okay, let me give you my address." She giggled again.

Andrew mentally gave himself a high five. He'd give this

address to Emma too. She could swing by and try to talk to the girlfriend face to face.

* * * * * * * * * *

Cari tried to remember what she was thinking about when she first got to the newsroom. Cardian's interruption had really sidetracked her train of thought. She tapped her pencil on her desk and it came to her. Bob had told her that there were eight athletes that Genevieve and her partner had interviewed. Cari thought she might be able to ferret out some of the names by looking into the newspaper's archived editions. She remembered interviewing a student last year who had broken the school record for most home runs in a season. At the time, it had seemed like a routine article. Newsworthy because records weren't broken every season, but not completely unexpected. She found the article and refreshed her memory. *Andrew Niles.*

A quick Google search revealed that Niles had had a successful high school baseball career. He hadn't broken any records, but he had hit more than his fair share of homers. His hometown paper had speculated that he would go to one of the big DI schools on a baseball scholarship. *So how did you end up at our private university, Mr. Niles?* She dug a little deeper and found a Facebook link to another local headline. Niles was quoted as saying that he had expected to sign with a DI school, but after meeting the baseball coach as well as various members of the athletic department, he had changed his mind. Cari skimmed the article some more and found what she had been looking for. Niles felt like the private school offered him the whole package and *even the sports medicine doctor is part of helping you achieve your goals.*

This wasn't solid evidence that Niles had been one of Delamont's athletes, but it seemed promising. She opened her notes document and added Niles to the list with Emma Savol and

140

Stephen Ithaca. She wished that she could get Marjorie to help her identify some of the others. Obviously, Genevieve wasn't going to share information with her. Cari opened another tab on her browser. She tried to come up with the right search parameters that would point her towards Delamont but might not mention his name. *What was it that Marjorie had said Stephen called the powder?* Nutritional supplement. She typed *nutritional supplement + sports medicine* along with the university's name into the search engine. As expected, it yielded thousands of results. Before narrowing her search options, she decided to click through a few links. The first four were completely unrelated and more like advertisements, but the fifth one was a news article from the Butler County Record. She didn't know where Butler County was, but the story mentioned a swimmer by the name of Casey Ryvers who had qualified for state in the 100-meter butterfly for two years in a row. The young woman was interviewed following a signing ceremony that her high school had hosted for all of the graduating seniors who received athletic scholarships for college. *"Getting a scholarship to swim in college has always been my dream. I knew this was the school for me after my first visit with the athletic department. I was treated like royalty; I not only met the athletic director, but also the chief sports medicine doctor. Everyone works together to help every athlete reach their highest potential."*

Cari went back to her own newspaper's archives and searched for Ryvers. Ms. Ryvers was a standout on the swim team. She was even named as one of the captains as a sophomore. Cari added Casey Ryvers to her growing list. Checking her watch, she realized that she'd worked through lunch already. She felt like she was on a roll and didn't want to quit. She continued sifting through the news articles and collecting names for her list. She wasn't sure how she was going to contact any of the students, but she'd worry about that later.

Cari had added five names to her list when she felt her cell phone buzz. She thought about letting it go to voicemail, but maybe it was Genevieve calling to apologize for being so rude and condescending last night. She pulled her phone from her pocket and saw Marjorie's name flashing on the screen. *It's about time,* she thought.

"Hi Marjorie! What's up?"

Cari strained to hear what she was saying. "Marjorie? Are you there? I can barely hear you."

"I want to talk to you. Can you meet me somewhere?"

"Marjorie, of course. Are you okay? Has something changed?"

"I can't right now. Please. Here's my address." She quickly reeled it off. "How soon can you be here?"

Cari was already grabbing her purse and double checking that her keys were in it. "I'm less than five minutes away. Are you safe? Should I call the police?"

"I'm fine. I just. Please hurry." She ended the call.

Cari raced out of her office and back to the parking garage. She wondered what had changed Marjorie's mind.

* * * * * * * * * *

Marjorie split the blinds on her window and peered out to the street below. The runner from Stephen's track team was still sitting at the bus stop bench across the street. Marjorie had started to leave to go to the library to study when she noticed Emma getting out of her car. Emma hadn't seen Marjorie come outside, so she ducked back into her building and climbed the stairs back to her apartment. The bus had pulled up soon after, but Emma didn't get on it. She had her cell phone out and was looking at Marjorie's apartment building.

Tiff had stopped home earlier, all excited because she had a date. Marjorie hadn't recognized the name and was concerned that Tiff had only just met the guy. Maybe he wasn't trustworthy. Tiff assured her that he was a perfect gentleman and that she'd be fine. He was picking her up for dinner and would drop her off at the ice cream parlor afterward. Marjorie knew that Tiff was very self-conscious. Her friend often sold herself short because she wasn't petite or slim. It was good to see her feeling so excited about a date. All of this had been running through her head as she'd stepped outside earlier. If the sunlight hadn't glinted off of Emma's car, she might not have seen her pull up.

She wondered when the newspaper woman would arrive. It had already been three and a half minutes since she'd called. Marjorie peeked through the blinds again just as a tan Toyota sedan pulled up in front of her building. She grabbed her purse and her apartment keys. She was wearing a grey hoodie and pulled the hood up over her head, hoping to disguise herself somewhat. Locking the door behind her, she quickly walked over to the car. She bent down to double-check that it was Cari Turnlyle and recognized her immediately from the track meet. She pulled open the passenger door and slid into the seat.

"Just drive somewhere. Anywhere." She told Cari. The woman nodded and put the car in gear. They pulled away from the curb. It was all Marjorie could do to not look back at Emma to see if she'd noticed.

* * * * * * * * *

Emma pulled up her phone and took a picture of the car Marjorie had just gotten into. It had a decal on the back window that looked like some sort of parking sticker. She enlarged the image to get a better look at the decal. *Brenington Beagle*. The newspaper woman! Emma vaguely remembered seeing a similar vehicle at the track on Saturday. The woman had just asked for Marjorie's phone number, but surely, she had talked to her already. Why would she be picking her up now? She texted Andrew that

Marjorie had left with a reporter. He had somehow gotten a date with Marjorie's roommate and was at dinner with her now. *Like a bunch of boomers catching the early bird.* She rolled her eyes. She texted Andrew again.

Find out how often M is talking to this reporter and why.

She was already walking to her car so that she could follow Marjorie and the reporter. Her car was on the opposite side of the street, so she needed to flip a U to get behind them. Looking up the street, she saw the tan sedan make a right turn towards the campus. She started the car and put it in gear while tugging on her seatbelt. Soon she was making the same right turn, but when she drove down the street towards campus, she didn't see any sign of the car Marjorie had gotten into. She clenched her fist in frustration. It was up to Andrew to get them information now.

* * * * * * * * * * *

Genevieve's desk phone rang again. It was Chris from CSU. She hoped that he'd gotten a hit on one of the phones they were keeping tabs on.

"Chris, tell me some good news."

"Good news, bad news again. I got a ping from Niles' phone, but it didn't last long. He turned it off after just a few minutes. I can't guarantee that he's still where he was."

"Better than nothing, Chris. Where was he? He could still be there." She signaled to Alex that they needed to be on the move.

"He was over by an apartment building near the university. It's not on-campus housing, but it's real close. Let me give you the address." He rattled off the address.

"Thanks, Chris. How long is your shift today? Is anyone coming in for a night shift?"

"I finish at seven tonight. I'm not sure. The chief's been trying to reduce hours lately. Budget cuts and all. I could show you how to run the application if you need to do it after I leave. Let me give you my cell phone number, so I can get in touch with you while you're away from the station."

"Thanks. I really appreciate it. Keep me posted." She quickly saved his number and then looked over at Alex.

"Where are we going?"

"Back over by the campus. Andrew Niles' phone placed him near an apartment building. He might still be there. Nothing on Hartfeld's phone yet."

"All right. Let's go see if we can find that kid." He tossed her the keys.

"Oh, you're gonna let me drive, huh?"

"I've noticed that you have a certain skill set that can be opportune for college campuses. Don't let it go to your head."

They hurried out to the car. Just as she was pulling away from the station, her cell phone buzzed with an incoming call. After seeing that it was Chris, she handed her phone to Alex, indicating that he should answer. Alex put it on speaker.

"What's up, Chris?"

"Hartfeld just turned his phone on. Looks like he's back at home, based on the address you gave me."

"Okay, great. We know where that is. We'll give him a call after we try to catch up with Niles. Thanks, Chris." Genevieve signaled to Alex to end the call.

"Why don't I just give him a ring again right now?" Alex offered.

"Go for it. Maybe we can catch him at home. We won't be far from there once we're at this other address."

Alex took out his own phone and dialed Hartfeld again. It rang several times, but the scientist eventually answered the call.

"Detective Runimoss, I presume?" Hartfeld asked.

"It's actually both of us, sir. Did you get my calls from earlier today?"

"Oh, yeah. I did. I forgot to return them. I was right in the middle of something and it just slipped my mind. How can I help you?"

"We had a few follow up questions that we'd like to ask you."

"Ask away, Detective."

"Actually, sir, we'd prefer to ask our questions in person. We can come to you or you can meet us at the station. Either way works." Alex offered.

"That sounds like an interrogation almost. I'm actually just on my way out. I'm meeting someone in a bit. Why don't you come by my office on campus tomorrow morning? I have a lecture at nine, but I'm free at ten for a few hours."

Alex looked at Genevieve, who nodded in agreement. "That sounds great. We'll be at your campus office tomorrow at ten a.m."

Hartfeld gave them the address of his office before ending the call. Alex put his phone away as Genevieve pulled up to the curb outside an apartment building. There were no other vehicles along the street on either side.

"Looks like we missed him. There's no telling where he went from here. Call Chris real quick and see if there is a car registered to Andrew Niles. We can put out a BOLO for it."

Genevieve grabbed her phone from the console where Alex had left it and pulled up Chris' number again. "Hey, Chris—what kind of car does the Niles kid drive? We were going to look around the area and see if he's nearby. If that fails, it's time to put out a BOLO for him."

"Let's see. I'm checking the DMV records. Do you know if he's a resident here or did he come from another state?"

Genevieve sighed. "I have no idea, Chris. Maybe we'll get lucky and there will only be one Andrew Niles in the country."

"I'm running the search. If we get a lot of results, I can easily check out his background from the school website. They list the hometowns of all the athletes." Genevieve could hear him tapping on the desk while his computer ran the search. "We also know his approximate age, so we can narrow it down that way too. Here we go. Seventeen names, but only one that's college-aged. He has a 2012 blue Chevy Impala registered in his name. I'll text you the license plate."

"Awesome. Blue should be easy to spot. Oh, by the way, you can cancel the screen on Hartfeld. We got him to answer his phone and set up a meeting for tomorrow."

"Roger that. I'll let you know if this other one pops up again." He ended the call.

"Blue Chevy Impala, Alex. Which way should I drive?" She asked as she put the car in gear again.

"Let's drive towards campus. Maybe he had a workout or team meeting. I requested a BOLO for the vehicle and attached my number to it. I just asked to be alerted; I didn't request that they pull him over or anything."

"Okay, good. He's still just a person of interest, though he's rapidly becoming a suspect in my mind."

"It is odd that he scheduled a meeting and then canceled it around the same time our vic was killed. He didn't mention that when I interviewed him either, which means he's hiding something."

Genevieve drove towards campus looking for any blue sedans along the way. Every vehicle she saw was either white, tan, or grey. They quickly reached the center of the university. She turned towards the gym.

"Where do we go if we don't see him on campus?"

"I guess we head back to the station again. We can go over what we want to ask Hartfeld and how we want to conduct the interview."

As they were passing the gymnasium, Genevieve happened to notice a familiar tan sedan parked along the curb. Just past the gym was the university's *Commons* or green space. She could just barely see it from the road. Looking past the car, she saw Cari sitting with a young woman on one of the park benches. *What are you up to, Cari Turnlyle?*

"Gen! Watch where you're going." Alex's outburst snapped her eyes back to the street. She had drifted into the middle and another car was approaching from the opposite direction.

"Sorry, I thought I saw something across the way." She steered the car back over to the right. "False alarm."

"Let's head back to the station then. Unless Niles turns his phone back on, we don't have a lot left to do today."

* * * * * * * * * *

Hartfeld unlocked his office and turned on the light. He needed to feed his hamsters and go over his notes for his lecture the next day. He was also supposed to meet one of his biochemistry students who had some questions about last week's lectures. Hartfeld looked at his watch. The student wasn't supposed to arrive for another fifteen minutes, so he had time to feed the hamsters first. He had turned his cell phone off earlier after getting another string of texts from the unknown number. The person had gotten increasingly more menacing in their messages. Hartfeld didn't know what the person was after exactly. He didn't even know who it was. He was just a biochemistry professor. He had never been threatened like this in his life. He pulled out his phone to read through the texts again.

The only way out is to work together.

Pick a meeting place and we can settle this. No one else has to know.

You're running out of time. The police are on to you. Give me what I want, or you'll regret it.

Listen, you piece of shit. I'm done playing nice. I will find you and I will get what I want.

Hartfeld shivered as he read the last one again. Who did this guy think he was? He was sure it was a man. He was also sure that it was not a college student. The person texted in complete sentences with punctuation. No one under twenty-five years old did that, but maybe it was a student trying to look like an adult. He thought about calling the police and telling them about the person harassing him. What could the police do, though? They would want to know what led the person to threaten him and he didn't know how to answer that question either. He didn't even know who it was. They'd probably just tell him that he was a paranoid, old man. They were *just* text messages after all.

He pulled out his biochemistry notebook and flipped through the lecture slides he had printed out years ago. This was an entry level class, so the information was basic and hadn't changed in ages. After refreshing his memory on the lecture, he closed the notebook and grabbed his keys again. He kept the hamster food in the same room, but he kept the powder locked in one of the cabinets. He locked his office and headed down the hallway to his lab.

Inside the hamsters' room, he went through the cages systematically to put fresh water in each bottle. It was the day that the selected hamsters got their nutritional supplement, so he unlocked the cabinet to get it out. As he was closing the door, he thought he heard the elevator ding down the hallway. Maybe the student had arrived early, but students shouldn't have access to the building on the weekends. Setting the container on the counter, he stuck his head out into the hallway to see who was there. He rarely saw anyone else on the weekend and especially not this late on a Sunday. Hartfeld looked up and down the hall but didn't see anyone. Frowning, he turned back to the hamsters and got to work measuring out the powder.

* * * * * * * * *

Andrew hadn't texted Emma back, so she decided to reach out to the whole group. It was really troubling to see Marjorie getting into the reporter's car. Emma thought back to her brief encounter with the newswoman. She had felt a little guilty about giving her Marjorie's number but hadn't realized the broader ramifications at the time. If Marjorie knew about the powder, would she tell the newswoman?

Hey everyone. Might have a problem. The GF just left with a newswoman.

She waited for someone to respond. If Marjorie told the newswoman about the powder, the program was over. They couldn't let that happen.

How did she get hooked up with a newswoman (Wiley)

If she tells the newspaper, we r screwed (Derek)

Has anyone talked 2 Whitham (Jess)

WTH is Andrew (Alan)

Emma didn't know what to do. She had lost track of the car and Marjorie. The texts kept pouring in. Everyone was agitated and worried. They all relied on the program to stay above their competition. Andrew had better be getting some information from that roommate!

* * * * * * * * * * *

Back at the station, Genevieve looked over her notes from their first interview with Hartfeld. He was an odd character, but wasn't that the stereotype for scientists? Absent minded and all that? He seemed a bit eccentric even. She read the rest of her notes and an idea hit her.

"Alex, I know we mentioned that Hartfeld didn't really give us an alibi, but you know what else he didn't do?"

"What?"

"He didn't ask *how* Delamont was killed. He used the word

murdered first. We just said that he was found dead in his office."

"True, but Delamont was in great shape and not old. It's a reasonably logical jump to suspect that he was killed rather than he had a health incident. It is a bit weird that he didn't ask how he was killed. I'll give you that."

"Yes, and taken with his convenient memory lapse about getting a call from our vic the night before his death makes him extra suspicious in my book."

"Equally suspicious as the Niles kid. I've never met a teenager who keeps their phone off this much."

"I think he's actually twenty years old, according to the DMV anyway. Not technically a teen."

Alex made a face at her. "Whatever. You know what I mean. Is he on a date or what? Every college and high school kid I've been around is constantly buried neck-deep in their phone. This kid's phone has been off for *hours* today. What gives?"

Just then, Alex's desk phone rang. He grabbed the receiver. "This is Runimoss." Pause. "Great, thank you." He replaced the receiver. "That was dispatch. They received a report of a blue Chevy Impala at a restaurant in Brenington, that Tex-Mex place."

"The one on campus?"

"No, the other one. Off campus. Should we go try to pick him up or wait for the morning?" He checked his watch. "It's already five o'clock. We weren't even supposed to work today. The LT is never going to approve all of this OT."

"I don't think he's a flight risk or anything, Alex. You said that he seemed pretty committed to the baseball team, right? It sounds like he must be on a date. We don't know that he's actually done anything wrong. I would hate to march him out of a restaurant just because he deleted a meeting request. Still, are we being irresponsible by not questioning him today?"

"You're right. We don't want to get into a position where we've brought undue suspicion on this kid. I think we have to call

it a night. Maybe he'll turn his phone on tomorrow and we can pick
him up for a second interview then."

Chapter 14

Cari drove Marjorie a few blocks from her apartment to the Commons. There were park benches they could sit on and it wasn't in full view of the road unless you were really looking. Marjorie kept looking around and checking all of the nearby sidewalks.

"Marjorie, what are you afraid of?"

She took a deep breath. "Earlier, I decided that I needed to study for my calc2 test that's this week. I wanted to get out of the apartment, so I thought I'd go to the library. Just as I stepped outside, I saw a car drive up across the street by the bus stop. The person driving it was Emma from the track team. I have never seen her over here, and it felt off—her being near my apartment. I rushed back inside and watched her from my window facing the street. She parked the car and then sat on the bus stop bench. Who drives to a bus stop like that? I think she was watching my apartment."

"But why? Why would she be watching your apartment?"

"I don't know! She called me the other day. She has *never* called me before. She acted like she was calling to see how I was doing, but it felt like she was trying to get information from me or something. It was just weird."

Cari thought about what Marjorie had said. "Marjorie, when we spoke on the phone yesterday, you said that you thought Delamont was killed because of the powder that Stephen was taking. You were afraid to talk about it and you didn't want me to write about it. What else do you know about it?"

"I told you everything I know. He got it once a month from Delamont. He called it a nutritional supplement."

"You thought it was steroids." Cari prodded.

"I did, but it wasn't. I remembered that Stephen had to undergo routine drug tests because of the school's NCAA status. He always passed, so it couldn't have been an illegal substance."

Cari considered this. "Okay, did he ever tell you if anyone else took the supplement? Was it the whole track team or the whole athletic department?"

"He didn't say anything about that. I didn't think to ask." She shrugged. "Are you going to write about this? It will just kill Stephen's parents if they read that he was doping or something."

"I don't want to tarnish Stephen's name. I also don't know enough about this powder or where it came from to write anything about it. I have a theory that Stephen was part of a program with other athletes at the school. A select group. Most likely the group of athletes that the detectives were interviewing yesterday."

"That must be it. That's why they're following me. They're afraid that I know. They're afraid that I'll ruin their little program!" She looked around frantically, but no one was watching them. A few students were throwing a frisbee to each other across the park from them, but other than that, the place was deserted.

"It's okay, Marjorie. I have a friend who's a detective. We can call her, get you some protection while they figure this out." She pulled her phone out.

"Protection? That seems extreme, doesn't it? If you call the police, they'll make Stephen look bad. He wasn't a bad person. He was so good." She choked back a sob.

"The police aren't out to get people or make them look bad. I know you loved Stephen; I hear it in your voice. We're not going to ruin his memory for you or his parents. Genevieve's a good detective. She can help."

At that moment, Cari's cell phone buzzed with an incoming call. She glanced down at the screen and saw Genevieve's name.

"Let me answer this quickly. This is my detective friend. I can put it on speaker if you want. Let me see why she's calling first."

Cari offered as she answered the call.

"This is Cari."

"I cannot believe you would talk to Lionel Cardian and leak part of this investigation! My partner and my boss are livid." Genevieve growled at her.

"Leaked? What?"

"Check your Twitter feed. *Sports Medicine Doctor's Death Linked to Mysterious Death of Student Athlete.* It's from the *Brenington Beagle.* It had to have been you that told Cardian. You couldn't get any information from me, so you stooped to work with Cardian."

"I didn't. I-I-I" Cari stammered. How could Cardian have made the connection? She slammed her palm into her forehead. She hadn't locked her workstation when Marjorie called. That jerk must have read her notes on her computer.

"Gen, I didn't leak anything. You didn't even tell me anything! Cardian must have snooped on my computer. I left the newsroom in a rush..." She looked up to see Marjorie answering her own phone. "You have to believe me, Gen. I wouldn't do that."

Cari pulled the phone away from her ear and spoke to Marjorie. "Do you want to meet with the police? I can set it up?"

Marjorie nodded, but went back to her own conversation.

"Gen, listen. I'm talking to Ithaca's girlfriend, Marjorie right now. She can tell you more, and I think it will help you fill in some of the missing pieces to this story."

"It's not a *story*, Cari! It's a murder investigation."

"Fine, Genevieve. I get it. You're upset. I'm trying to fix it. Please believe me; I did not leak this to Cardian."

"Fine, where are we meeting?"

"How about that Tex-Mex place on campus?"

Cari scribbled *Tex-Mex?* on a scrap of paper and held it up to Marjorie. She agreed. "That works for us. Twenty minutes?"

After squaring away the details with Genevieve, Cari ended the call and waited for Marjorie to finish. She caught fragments of the young woman's conversation. It sounded like she was checking in with someone. Cari wondered if it was Stephen's parents or maybe her roommate. Before Marjorie hung up, Cari's phone buzzed with another incoming call. *Bob?!*

"Hey, Bob, what's up?"

"Cari, how could you? I could lose my job for this!"

"Bob, what are you talking about?"

"The tweet! You told Lionel Cardian what I said about the investigation. His series of tweets includes an *anonymous statement from someone within the ME's office.* Everyone will know that's me! Thanks a lot. I thought we were friends." He hung up.

Cari sighed. Cardian had really overstepped this time. He was burning through all of her contacts. Sure, she shouldn't have recorded Bob without his knowledge, but she had no intention of using any of his quotes. She just needed the information! *Damn you, Cardian!* Marjorie broke into her thoughts.

"Sorry, that was my roommate. She went on a date with someone she just met today and I made her promise to check in with me when she got to the restaurant. I was worried that the guy wasn't who she thought he was. You can never be too careful."

"That's really kind of you to look out for her."

"We look out for each other. You know how it is. So, what's the story with your police friend? I told my roommate that I'd be at the Tex-Mex restaurant since you mentioned it. She has to work tonight and is going there straight from her date. I didn't want her to worry if she came home early though and I wasn't there."

"You have a great sense of keeping yourself safe. I'm impressed."

"My mom has ingrained this in me since I was a child. Never go anywhere alone, well, I break that one a lot, but I always tell someone where I'm going. I was usually going somewhere with

Stephen, but I always told Tiff too. Just a good habit, you know? That was the other rule, always tell someone where you're going."

"I told Genevieve we'd meet her there in about fifteen minutes. It's not too far from here."

Marjorie's face got serious. "I don't know how to talk to the police. It feels like I'm in trouble or something."

"Genevieve is not going to make you uncomfortable. I promise."

"I almost forgot. Your friend called you. She sounded upset. What was that about?"

Cari bit her lip. "Oh, it was nothing. A misunderstanding. We worked it out, but I do need to send a text to someone before we leave for the restaurant."

Cari looked at her phone and scrolled through her contacts to her boss' name. She selected it and composed a text message.

Cardian does not know what he's talking about. You need to pull that tweet before we get in trouble.

She waited for her boss to respond, but instead her phone buzzed with an incoming call. She rotated her body away from Marjorie.

"Boss, if you haven't heard from someone else already, get ready for some calls. Cardian went to Twitter with some of *my* research and he doesn't know the whole story. He's causing problems that are not going to be good for the paper." She told him before he could speak.

"Turnlyle, what in the world? Are you accusing Cardian of stealing your story? I *told you* not to butt into his story."

"Sir, with all due respect, I am not butting in. I'm following *my* story. Regardless, you have to remove that tweet. It's not substantiated."

"Fine, but we're having a meeting about this tomorrow morning. I do not like how this is playing out." He ended the call. Cari waited a minute then pulled up her Twitter feed to double check that the tweets were gone, then she slid her phone back into her purse.

"Are you sure everything is okay?"

"Everything is fine. Are you ready to meet Genevieve, uh, Detective Viacorte?"

Chapter 15

Tiffany walked back to the table and slipped her phone into her purse. The waitress had brought their food while she was speaking with Marjorie on the phone. Andrew was waiting for her to return to start eating. *What a gentleman!*

"I'm sorry for keeping you waiting!" She exclaimed as she slid back into the booth.

"No problem at all." He smiled at her. "Is everything okay with your roommate?"

"I think so. She's had a really hard time lately. I'm trying to make sure that she's taking care of herself. Her boyfriend died on Friday."

"Oh wow! That's crazy. Was he sick or...?" Andrew asked.

"I don't think so. He was on the track team. Did you hear about it? You're an athlete here, right?"

"You know, I think I did hear something about that. That was your roommate's boyfriend?" He asked incredulously.

"Yeah, it's so tragic. It really rocked her, but she's been strong through it all. She's escorting his parents around to different things and plans to go to classes tomorrow. I don't know how she does it."

"Did she say what caused his death? Sorry, maybe that's none of my business." He said sheepishly.

"You know, I don't think they really know. I did overhear her say that they hadn't released his body to his parents yet."

"That's strange. We weren't told that anything suspicious had happened. I wonder what's going on."

"Yeah, I have no idea. This morning, or was it yesterday? It doesn't matter. She closed her door to talk to someone on the phone. I found out later that it was a reporter! I didn't press her on it, but it was kind of surprising. I guess it helps to talk to someone, even if it's the media." She shrugged.

"The newspaper? Like the *Brenington Beagle*?"

"The very one. Some lady has called her several times over the weekend to talk to her. In fact, she's going to dinner with her later tonight at that other Tex-Mex place on campus." She scrunched up her face.

"What?"

"I was just replaying our conversation in my mind. She said that the newspaper lady was bringing along her friend who's with the police. Surely that's not right. Why would Marjorie need to talk to the police?" Tiffany noticed a brief note of alarm on Andrew's face that quickly disappeared.

"Maybe something to do with why they haven't released the body?"

"Oh, maybe so." She took another bite.

"It's really great of you to look after your roommate. I'm sure she needs someone to lean on right now." He reached across the table and grabbed her hand, squeezing it gently.

Tiffany blushed. "Thank you. She's a really great person and anyone would do the same in my shoes."

He released her hand. "I need to run to the restroom. I'll be right back. Oh! And if the waitress brings the check while I'm gone, don't you dare pay for it. This is *my* treat." He winked at her.

* * * * * * * * * * *

Andrew tried to walk casually to the bathrooms. It took all of his willpower not to pull his phone out before he entered the men's room. He needed to text the group that Ithaca's girlfriend was meeting with the police! That couldn't be a good sign. He turned on his phone and sent a message to the group.

GF has arranged to meet with police! Tonight. Casa Rosarita on campus.

He tapped his foot, trying to will someone to respond. He couldn't very well drive over there now. Besides, he was supposed to be taking Tiffany to work. He rolled his eyes. This date could not end soon enough. Finally, an incoming text from Jess.

I'm on it. I'll head over there now and try to eavesdrop on the conversation.

Andrew breathed a sigh of relief. What would they do if the girl knew about the powder and told the police, though? Before he could think of a solution, another text appeared.

If it sounds like she's going to talk about the powder, cause a commotion or something. (Derek)

Andrew nodded to himself in agreement. They needed to find a way to keep that girl from talking to the police. Just the fact that she *wanted* to talk to the police meant that she knew something. He turned his phone off again and slipped it back into his pocket.

* * * * * * * * * *

Tiffany smiled at Alex when he returned from the men's room. She was finished eating and wasn't going to order dessert. Working at the ice cream parlor when your stomach was too full was the worst. She'd learned that early on. She casually glanced at her watch as he sat back down.

"Where did you say you work again?" He asked.

"The little ice cream parlor on campus. It's just a few minutes from here, I think."

"I bet that's a fun job to have. Do you get free samples or discounted tubs of ice cream?"

"There's an employee discount, but I try not to take advantage of it. I have a scholarship here for my classes, but it doesn't cover my rent or my food plan or any other living expenses, like the textbooks! Digital or not, those are expensive." She sighed.

"Right? Feels like price gouging sometimes." He signaled to the waitress for the check. "Let me know how your roommate is doing. The athletic program at Onore is really a great one. Even though she's not on a team, she's still part of our community. I'm sure that I speak for everyone when I say that we wouldn't want her to feel deserted."

"That's so kind of you, Andrew. I'll keep you posted for sure."

* * * * * * * * * * *

Genevieve had barely gotten home when her lieutenant called, angry that the newspaper was connecting the two deaths. It was the first he'd heard about it and *why* hadn't she mentioned it and *who* had leaked this to the press? She couldn't answer any of the questions, but she had an idea. Cari had been chasing that story, that *connection* between the deaths.

Her friend had sounded truly surprised to learn about the tweet. Still, Genevieve wondered if Cari wasn't working all the angles in an effort to chase down this story of hers. Didn't they realize that lives were at stake? At least she had talked her source into meeting with the police. Genevieve hadn't told Alex about the meeting. It sounded like the young woman was pretty scared already and Alex was a fairly intimidating presence. She could call him in later.

After speaking with Cari, she had immediately gotten back in her car to drive straight to the restaurant. She hoped that the casual atmosphere would help their witness relax and talk to them. She had asked Cari for twenty minutes even though it only took her about twelve to get to the restaurant. She wanted to get there first and get a table in the back, away from the busyness. On her way there, she had gotten another call from Chris that Niles had turned his phone back on. He was on the move. It sounded like he was driving back to campus. Genevieve asked Chris to keep the system active on the athlete's phone, but unless he looked to be heading out of town, they weren't going to try to catch up with him tonight. Genevieve requested a table for three and ordered water for everyone. She sat facing the entrance, watching for Cari to enter. After a few minutes, a tall, young woman entered. She inwardly berated herself for not finding out what the girlfriend looked like from Cari first. She was black with her dark hair pulled back into a low ponytail. Genevieve started to wave her over, then realized that she recognized her from yesterday's interviews—Jess Loster. Genevieve was thankful that she'd sat in the back and that the family in the neighboring booth shielded her from Jess' line of sight. Was it a coincidence that one of the athletes arrived at the restaurant just minutes before her witness? Frustrated, she called Cari.

"Hey. Change of plans. I think we have an unwelcome guest here. Let's meet somewhere else. Gotta run." She ended the call and left a five on the table for the waitress' troubles. She held up her phone to her face to conceal her identity somewhat in case Jess looked up as she passed her table. Thankfully, the young woman was watching the door, so her back was to Genevieve. She slipped past her, confident that Jess hadn't seen or at least hadn't recognized her.

Leaving the restaurant, she got back into her car to call Cari back. She hadn't expected to see a familiar face and wasn't sure what it meant. Cari answered her call immediately.

"What's going on? Who was at the restaurant?"

"One of the athletes that I interviewed yesterday. It could be a coincidence, but..."

"I thought coincidences were no big deal." Cari retorted, immediately regretting it. "I'm sorry, that was uncalled for."

Genevieve took a breath and pursed her lips. "As I was saying, maybe she just happened to be there, but my gut says it's more than that. Where can we meet instead?"

"Let me see what Marjorie wants to do." Cari covered her

microphone and whispered to Marjorie for a few minutes. "Let's go back to the Commons at the university. It's outside and we can easily see if anyone is approaching us."

* * * * * * * * * * *

Cari glanced at Marjorie after turning her car back towards Onore. The girl was fidgeting with her hands and looked really rattled. She wondered if she was considering not talking with the police after all.

"Is everything okay? You seem upset." Cari observed.

"You said that the detective—your friend—saw someone from the athletic department at the restaurant? Are they following me? How could they know I was going there?"

"It could just be a coincidence. The police can only help. It's good that you want to talk to them." She encouraged. *Plus, maybe I can get a little more information from Genevieve about the other side of this case if I bring her a key witness!*

"I don't know. It feels like I'm being watched or followed wherever I go. First outside my apartment, then they were at the restaurant too. Maybe I just need to let this all go. Let Stephen's memory rest as it is. I think I want to go home. I don't think I can do this."

Cari panicked. She didn't want to lose this opportunity. "Are you sure? The police can protect you. They are public servants, right? They won't manipulate you." She cringed as she realized that she was doing just that to the poor young woman.

"No. I can't do it. Please take me home. My roommate will be there later. She gets off at like nine. That's just a few hours from now. I'll lock the door, and close the blinds. I won't let anyone else in."

It took all of Cari's mental strength not to let her shoulders sag. "Okay. It's your call. If you change your mind, you know how to reach me, right?"

Marjorie nodded as Cari flipped another U and drove towards the apartment building for the second time that day. "Please tell your friend that I'm sorry."

"I will," Cari said as she pulled up alongside the curb. "Text me when you're safely inside. I'll wait here until I hear from you."

Marjorie looked around the building and when she didn't see anyone, she quickly exited the car. She took the steps two at a time and was inside the building in just a few seconds. Cari pulled up Genevieve's number and called her again.

"Hey. Bad news. Marjorie got spooked by you seeing that athlete at the restaurant. She had me take her back home. She's too scared to talk to the police." She heard Genevieve groan.

"Ugh! We can protect her. I mean, I don't really have a budget for that, but I know we can work something out. I can request that a squad car patrol her street. If she's scared, then she really needs to talk to me."

"I know, but she's not ready. I really wish that she was." She sighed. "She just texted me that she's inside and she locked her door."

"I can't get someone to patrol her street if she isn't working with us."

"I know that. Thankfully, no one is out here right now. Her roommate will be back in a few hours. They look out for one another. She should be fine, right?"

"What does she know that puts her in such danger, Cari?"

"You know I can't tell you that. I can't betray her."

"I could charge you both with obstruction."

"You wouldn't dare. You wouldn't even *know* about Marjorie if I hadn't told you about her." She ended the call.

Cari checked her surroundings again but didn't see a soul. Hopefully, no one was actually looking for Marjorie and her young friend was just being paranoid. She put her car in gear and pulled away from the curb. She wondered if Cardian was still in the newsroom. She needed to get her workstation shut down before anyone else snooped on it too. It made her so angry that he'd try to steal from her. What a jerk! Plus, he'd jeopardized her friendship with Bob. She needed to call Bob and apologize.

Please pick up, please pick up, Cari thought as the call went through her car's Bluetooth feature. She heard a click and started to say hi to Bob when she recognized his voicemail.

Hey, it's Bob. Leave a message. Beep.

She smiled at his corny message and actually saying *beep* before the voicemail beeped. "Hey, Bob. It's Cari. Bob, you have to believe me; I did *not* tell Cardian that you spoke to me. I wouldn't do that. You know me. I wouldn't do anything to hurt you. Please forgive me. Please call me back. I want to make this right."

She ended the call and focused on getting back to her desk. Hopefully, Cardian was already gone; she really didn't want to put up with his shenanigans. She realized that she was clenching her jaw as tightly as she was gripping the steering wheel and willed herself to relax. This was just another one of life's hurdles. She would get over it and be stronger for it.

Ten minutes later, she parked in the parking garage again. Cardian's BMW was still in his spot nearest the entrance. She rolled her eyes. He probably cheated his way up to the front page. Her hands clenched into fists just thinking about his arrogance.

She entered the newsroom and looked around to see who was still working. Sure enough, she could see the top of Cardian's toupee sticking out from above the cubicle walls. She wouldn't confront him yet. She wanted to check out her workstation first. As she approached her desk, she saw that the computer screen was off. She knew that she'd left it on in her haste to get to Marjorie. She looked at the CPU below the desk. The light was still on, indicating that it was running. She reached forward and pushed the power button on the monitor. The screen blinked to life and showed her page of notes about Ithaca and the athletes. She couldn't prove that Cardian had been the one to look at her notes, but she suspected he was guilty. She tapped her fingers on her desk as she tried to decide how best to proceed. Her thoughts were interrupted by a knock on her cubicle wall.

"You rushed out of here in a hurry earlier. Get a break in the story?"

Cari whipped her head around. *Cardian!* "It seems like you're being extra observant of my habits, Lionel." She smiled at him but knew that he could see the anger in her eyes.

"Bit of temper on you, huh? I told our dear ole' boss that you were over-reaching your assignment. He found that *quite* interesting."

"And what would make you think that, *Lionel?*" She spat out his name, unable to fully hide her anger.

"Now, now. A good journalist leaves no stone unturned when chasing his story. Thank you for letting me in on your little theory about the deaths being related. I don't read the sports section ever, so I never would have known that there were two deaths on campus if you hadn't told me."

"I didn't tell you anything and you *know* it!" She raised her voice.

The newsroom was mostly deserted, but unfortunately, not completely deserted. Cari's outcry had alerted the attention of the only other person working on a Sunday evening: her editor.

"What in tarnation?" He asked as he approached her desk. "Miss Turnlyle, I told you that this was Lionel's story and not to overstep your assignment. It seems that you had information that could have helped him out, but you kept it to yourself. Is that what I'm hearing?"

Cari froze. *How dare he turn this around on her!* "Sir, I-I-uh, I—"

"As I was just saying, *sir,*" Cardian's voice mimicked Cari's, "she *did* share her research with me. That's what led me to make that tweet that you felt inclined to delete."

"Why am I the last to hear about this? Miss Turnlyle, I do NOT like being kept in the dark. I need to know what you're up to before you're up to it. I can find a new sports reporter faster than you can make a layup." He stomped off towards his office as Cardian chuckled at her unfortunate circumstances.

"Anything else you need to share with me, sweetheart?" He said sarcastically.

She narrowed her eyes at him. "No. I think you have everything you need. This is not a game, though, Lionel. Please don't play fast and loose with this."

"It sure sounds like you know more than you're telling me."

"Unlike some people in this newsroom, I know how to protect a source. And right now, that's where it stands. I can't share that with you."

"We're supposed to be on the same team here, Turnlyle. The team that sells newspapers. Or did you forget?"

"I'm done talking with you, Lionel. If and when my source wants to share with you, you'll be the first to know." She turned back to her screen and saved her document. Then she closed her other tabs and shut down the computer.

"Leaving so soon?" He asked.

She ignored him and gathered up her belongings. She was almost shaking, she was so angry, but she fought to keep her composure. She wouldn't let him see that he'd gotten to her. She pushed her chair in and walked right past him to the exit.

* * * * * * * * * *

Andrew looked at his phone and ran his hand over his face. This nightmare just kept spiraling out of control. The girl didn't show at the restaurant! Now they didn't know where she was *again.*

Ithaca's roommate was a no show at my study session. (Wiley)

Great! Andrew couldn't believe how terrible their luck was. It should be easy to keep track of one girl and find out if her boyfriend talked too much. Why was this so hard? He sent his own text.

GF's roommate said that she would keep me updated

It seemed likely that the girl would return to her apartment. Maybe Emma should go back and wait for her. Emma seemed pretty convinced that she had spooked the girl even though she didn't think she'd been seen. He clenched his right hand into a fist. The girl could be talking to the police right now! *Where was she?* His phone buzzed with another incoming text.

Powder is secured. Program is back on. New pick-up schedule pending for tomorrow.

Andrew cocked his head to one side. How did this happen? He didn't really trust this contact but didn't want to cross the person either. Before he could respond, another text showed up on his screen.

What is the girl's story? What does she know?

Andrew sighed. It was probably better to call, but he didn't want to get yelled at again. He thumbed off a response.

Story still unknown.

Just as he expected, the person immediately called Andrew's phone. His thumb hovered over the decline call button. He wished he had the nerve to ignore the caller.

"It's Andrew." He answered in a defeated tone.

"What seems to be the hold up with the girl?"

"We're working on it. How did you get the powder back?"

"That's not something you need to worry about. You have one job right now. Talk to the girl. Find her or I will." The call ended.

Andrew felt a chill go up his spine. He didn't like the implications that were rolling through his mind. What had he gotten himself into?

* * * * * * * * * *

Cari was still trembling when she got back to her car. The nerve of Cardian, not only stealing her work but trying to manipulate her too, was maddening. On top of that, her editor was on Cardian's side. She had worked so hard to get her foot in the door of the newspaper business. It felt like everyone was working against her to take away her dream. She turned on her car and double-checked that her cell phone was connected to the Bluetooth feature. She wanted to call her grandmother while she drove back to her apartment.

Cari scrolled through the list of names once she had driven to the exit of the parking garage. She selected her grandmother's name and pressed the enter button on her steering wheel. The ringing sound reverberated through her car.

"Cari, my dear! How are you?"

"I'm so frustrated, Grandmother. I'm trying to write this story and it feels like I just keep running into a brick wall."

"What happened, sweetheart?"

Cari sighed. "The lead news writer snooped through my notes because I stupidly left my computer unlocked earlier today. Then my editor got mad because he thought I was trying to steal the guy's story. He implied that he might fire me! What's worse is that the information he leaked on Twitter came from my friend Bob, so now Bob isn't speaking to me. My best source to what's going on is too scared to talk about it and my friend on the police force doesn't really believe me anyway. Everywhere I turn, I just keep getting shut down. Maybe I was wrong. Maybe I'm not cut out to be a hot-shot newspaper writer." A tear leaked out of her left eye.

"Oh, Cari, my dear. Take a deep breath. You know, life is often referred to as a journey down a path towards some unknown destination. As you walk down this path, inevitably at some point, you find yourself in the forest. In every direction you look, there are trees, trees, and more trees. How did you get here? How do you get out? Which way is the right way? In that moment, you feel hopelessly and utterly lost. But in that moment, you have a choice. You can choose to keep moving forward and hope that you find a way out—a way through, or you can stop and give up. The choice is yours, my dear."

Cari's lips trembled as she tried to respond. She didn't want to give up her dream. She fingered her locket. Grandmother was right. She wasn't a quitter. "Thank you, Grandmother. Thank you so much. I'm going to find my way out of this mess and be better for it. I love you, Grandmother."

"I love you more, sweetheart."

Cari flipped a U in the middle of the street, causing an oncoming vehicle to blare its horn at her. She threw up a hand in apology. It was time to talk to Marjorie again.

Chapter 16

Marjorie sat on her bed and clasped her hands in her lap. It was the only way to keep them from shaking. Less than three days ago, everything had been so perfect. Well, maybe not perfect, but it was a hell of a lot better than it was right now. Stephen was dead, people were following her, and she'd just skipped out on a meeting with the police. *Could you get arrested for that?* She didn't know who to trust. Sighing, she realized that she hadn't updated Tiffany on her whereabouts. She pulled her phone out of her purse and unlocked it.

Hey Tiff. Decided to skip the restaurant meeting. Too tired.

She felt guilty lying to her friend, but she didn't want to get into it. Plus, Tiff was working and she didn't need to scare her with unnecessary details. She slipped her phone into her purse and laid back on her bed. Maybe now would be a good time to take another bubble bath. Tiff most likely wouldn't be home for at least two hours. She could make some hot chocolate and soak in the tub while she read a new crime novel. She felt herself nodding in agreement. Before she could get off the bed, her phone buzzed with an incoming call. *Tiffany.*

"Hey Tiff! I didn't mean for you to call."

"Are you okay? Did you at least eat dinner?"

"I had few snacks and some water. I'm fine. Aren't you at work?"

"It's a slow night. Too cold for ice cream, I guess. Why did you bail on the meeting with the police?"

Marjorie sighed. "I...well, you see, I...I think someone is having me followed." There, she said it.

"What?!"

"Maybe I'm being paranoid. It's just that Stephen's death has really thrown me for a loop. I think he was involved with something that he shouldn't have been."

"What?! Like drugs? I thought you said he wasn't like that."

"NOT drugs. I don't know. It's just. He was in this nutrition program…"

"What kind of program?"

"I'm not supposed to say anything." She hesitated.

"That sounds suspicious! What in the world?"

"They gave him this protein powder supplement thing. He swore it wasn't steroids, but now he's dead! I don't know. I shouldn't have told you. I just don't know what to think anymore."

"Marjorie! Did you tell the police? What if it was poison?"

"Oh, don't be so dramatic, Tiff. It couldn't have been poison. He's been taking it since August. I didn't meet with the police, remember?"

"Don't you think you should?"

"What if they find out that Stephen did something wrong? He was a good person, Tiff. He doesn't deserve to have his memory tarnished like this."

"But what if someone else gets hurt? Oh, shoot. Someone just walked in. I have to go. I'll try to call back later."

"Don't worry about me—" Marjorie tried to tell her before the call ended. She set the phone down and decided it was definitely time for a nice long soak in the bathtub.

Marjorie kicked off her shoes and socks, grabbed her book, and then went into the kitchen. She would warm up some milk in the microwave and then go start the bathtub while she mixed the cocoa powder into the mug. As she passed her bedroom, she heard her phone chime with an incoming text but chose to ignore it. Whoever it was could wait.

* * * * * * * * * *

Genevieve thought about calling Alex to tell him about her interactions with Cari. She knew that he didn't approve of her friendship with a member of the press. *Friendship?* She thought of Cari as a friend but realized there wasn't much substance to their relationship. In fact, it seemed like the two of them were just using each other to try to gather information. She shook her head. Regardless of Cari's profession, they could still be friends. It would just take a little effort on both their parts.

She swiped through the various apps on her phone, trying to consider this case from various angles as she mindlessly looked through Facebook and Instagram. The images on the screen sailed past faster than she was able to really see them. She closed all the apps and set her phone down. Someone had killed John Delamont, but who? And why? It felt like they hadn't made any progress on the case and it had almost been two days. She mentally went through all of their potential suspects. Hartfeld had lied about talking to Delamont the evening before he was killed, Whitham had a list of financial troubles a mile long, and Niles had tried to hide that he had scheduled a meeting with the victim.

Cari was certain the deaths were related, but she was holding on to some scrap of a clue from the girlfriend. Genevieve thought about the nutrition program again. The athlete that Cari was obsessed with had also been part of the so-called nutrition program. He had died unexpectedly, the cause was currently unknown, but the ME considered it to be an accident. Genevieve had to agree with Cari on one thing: the dead athlete did have a relationship with their victim. Maybe there was more to this case than she had previously assumed.

* * * * * * * * * *

Marjorie was startled to hear Tiffany's voice in the apartment already. She didn't think she had been soaking in the bathtub for two hours! The water would have gotten ice cold if that were the case and it was still quite hot. She marked her place in her book and set it aside. What was Tiff saying? Who was she talking to? She strained to hear over the bathroom fan.

"...steroids...No!! It wasn't...no...really spooked her...she's still here."

Marjorie's eyes grew big as she listened to Tiff's words. She pulled the drain on the bathtub and quickly wrapped a towel around herself to dry off. She had to get out of here and fast! She ripped open the door and almost walked right into Tiffany.

"Who are you talking to, Tiff?"

Tiffany pulled the phone away from her ear. "What? Oh. Andrew, the guy I went to dinner with. He's an athlete too! Did I tell you that? He was really concerned about you when I told him about Stephen and everything. He said that the athletic department—"

Marjorie cut her off. "What have you *done?!*"

Tiffany looked at her with wide, confused eyes as Marjorie pushed past her and slammed the door to her room closed. She grabbed a duffel bag and started throwing a few things in while also getting dressed. Her phone, where was her phone? On the bed! She grabbed it and thumbed off a text to the reporter. She hoped the woman wouldn't think she was like the boy who cried wolf. She couldn't stay here. Marjorie zipped the bag closed and threw the strap over her shoulder.

"Where are you going, Marjorie? What's wrong?" Tiff pulled the phone away from her ear again.

"Don't talk to me and whatever you do, do *not* open this door no matter who you think it is on the other side. I told you about Stephen in *confidence* and you just betrayed him and me! How could you, Tiff?" Marjorie cried as she grabbed her keys off the kitchen table and ran out the door. She had texted the reporter to pick her up outside but that she'd be heading towards the campus

175

police building.

Marjorie looked around as she dashed outside of her apartment building. She didn't see any familiar faces or vehicles. Campus police were only a few blocks away; she intended to run there as fast as she could. She gripped the duffel bag's strap firmly and took off. It was dark out now. She was so intent on getting to campus police, that she didn't notice a blue car turning onto her street.

Chapter 17

Cari was already halfway to Marjorie's apartment when she got her text. She tried to call Marjorie, but it went straight to her voice mail. Cari decided to get Genevieve on the phone too. She hadn't run that idea by Marjorie, but the young woman had said that she was heading towards Onore's campus police building, so she was probably okay with it. Genevieve answered immediately.

"Cari! Did you change her mind?"

"I need you to get back to campus ASAP. Marjorie's in trouble. I don't know what's going on. Meet us at campus police."

"What? Cari, this is the last time I'm chasing you around the campus. I'm not at your beck and call."

"Genevieve! Trust me on this. You *have* to come. She is scared. I don't know what happened. She just texted me. Stay on the line. I'm almost there."

"How are you almost there? You live at least ten minutes from campus!"

"I was hoping to get her to talk to me and change her mind about talking to you. I started driving over here, and then I got this frantic text that she needed me to pick her up."

Cari whipped around the corners, pushing the speed limit a bit. She was just two blocks away from the building now and all of the intersections had four-way stops. She slammed to a stop at the first one and was getting ready to gun it again when a blue car tore around the corner ahead of her. *The nerve of some people!* She thought about honking her horn at the inconsiderate driver, but before she could, the car skidded to a halt alongside the curb. The driver jumped out right in front of Cari's car. Her tires squealed in protest as she screeched to a stop, barely avoiding the young man who had just hopped up onto the sidewalk in a dead sprint.

Cari swerved around his still open door and strained to see what would cause him to abandon his vehicle in such a careless way. Suddenly, her heart lurched into her throat. *Marjorie!* She saw the girl sprinting across the grass towards the campus police building just up the block. The young man was fast and gaining on her. Cari honked once, hoping to distract him and get Marjorie's attention at the same time.

There was a small parking lot for the officers to use next to the building. Cari just needed to beat this hooligan to it. She pressed down on the gas pedal and flashed her lights as she whipped the car into the lot. She threw the car into park and reached across to open her passenger door. Marjorie jumped into the car as Cari put it into reverse and wheeled around back into the street. Her chest was heaving as she exhaled. Marjorie had tears streaming down her face.

"What just happened? Who are you running from?"

Genevieve's voice broke into Cari's thoughts before Marjorie could respond. "Cari! Cari! What is happening? I heard brakes squealing and tires skidding. People are crying. I'm maybe a minute away. Talk to me!"

Marjorie still couldn't speak. Cari drove past the blue car that still had its door open and sped off towards her own apartment. She tried to take a deep breath to slow down her heart rate.

"I was driving over to the campus police building when this guy came out of nowhere and cut me off. Then, he jumped out of his blue car and took off on foot. Turns out, he was chasing after Marjorie too! She's in the car now. I don't know where the young man is."

"I think I'm just passing you now."

Headlights flashed at Cari. She flashed hers back to show her recognition. "I'm taking Marjorie to my apartment. If you can find that young man, you need to figure out who he is and what his deal is. Call me back when you're headed my way." She hung up.

"Marjorie, are you okay? Deep breaths, relax. You're okay. You're safe. What happened? Who was that?"

"I don't know! I was at home and then Tiffany got home and then I overheard her on the phone and she was telling this guy about Stephen—about everything! I panicked and sent you a text, then started running for campus police. I didn't know what else to do."

"It's okay." Cari let out a big breath. "So, Tiffany is your roommate, right?"

Marjorie nodded.

"She went on a date with some new guy..."

"That's who she was talking to on the phone. He's another athlete. She said he was concerned about me, but I think she told him about the powder. It just felt all wrong. Why would some random athlete care about some dead guy's girlfriend?" She burst into tears again.

Cari reached into her console and handed Marjorie a tissue. "Remember, deep breaths. You're safe. Genevieve is going to find that guy and we're going to figure all of this out."

* * * * * * * * * *

Genevieve turned onto the street where the university's campus police office was located. She checked her watch; it had only been ninety seconds since she had heard Marjorie slam Cari's car door as they were driving away. No one else had passed her since she saw Cari driving by. Cari had said that it was a blue car. It had to be Niles, but where had he gone now? She turned left and saw brake lights ahead. She punched the dial for her car's Bluetooth and got Alex on the line.

"What now?" He answered.

"Quick! What's the license plate for Niles' car?"

"What? Where are you?"

"The license plate. Alex!" She growled at him.

"Chill. Let me look it up."

"Hurry. I don't want to follow the wrong car."

He read off the plate number to her. "Where are you?"

"I'm just about to drive away from campus. I'm not sure where he's headed, but I am going to make a traffic stop. We're approaching the intersection of Craft Avenue and Second Street."

"I'll be there in five minutes. You got your siren with you?"

"Just putting it up top." She answered as the blaring noise drowned out her last words. She ended the call and watched the car ahead of her. Would Niles run or would he cooperate?

* * * * * * * * * * *

Andrew slammed the palm of his hand into his steering wheel. *Damnit!* Not only had he lost the girl, but now he was getting pulled over too. Where had the cop come from? He hadn't even been speeding, had he? He pulled over to the curb. No sense making this worse than it was. Maybe his taillight was out. It was a pretty old car. That was probably it. He wiped his palms onto his jeans and tried to relax. He looked into his rearview mirror and his heart sunk. The cop from the other day, Detective what's-her-name, was walking towards his car. He hit the button to lower his window and sighed.

"Andrew Niles, right?" The short detective had a flashlight pointed at his face.

He squinted into the light. "Yes, ma'am, uh, Detective, sir—ma'am." He stuttered.

"Detective Viacorte." She smiled at him, but her eyes didn't look friendly. "I need you to step out of the car. Nice and slow."

"What? Uh? Should I call someone?"

"Who did you need to call, Mr. Niles?" She cocked her head

to one side with a glint in her eye as she continued to grin at him. "Like a lawyer?" He drew the words out slowly.

"I don't know, Mr. Niles. Do you think you need a lawyer?" Still with the grin.

He tried to relax but had never been pulled over before. "I don't know what I've done wrong."

"Why don't you step out of the car and we can chat about it? My partner should be here any minute."

He slowly unfastened his seatbelt and let the strap slide through his fingers. His shoulders dropped as he opened the door. This couldn't be good.

* * * * * * * * * *

Cari led Marjorie up to her apartment. The young woman was still sniffling a bit, but seemed to be holding up okay. She hoped that they would hear from Genevieve soon. Cari unlocked the door and pushed it open.

"This is my place. It's a little messy. Um, I don't get a lot of visitors." She said sheepishly as she quickly gathered up the stack of Chinese take-out boxes that lined the coffee table. She dumped them into the kitchen trash, which also had a terrible smell. She cringed. *Was she really such a slob?*

"Marjorie, have seat on the sofa. I'm just going to tidy up a bit."

"It's okay. You know I'm in college, right?" She smiled.

Cari laughed. "That I do. I don't want to be inhospitable. It will just take a moment."

She pulled the garbage bag from the kitchen trash and cinched it closed. After setting that by the door to take to the garbage chute, she looked into the bathroom to see its status. Her running clothes were discarded in a pile on the floor and there were several hairs in the sink. Toothpaste also dotted the countertop in multiple places. Of course, there were no paper towels handy, so glancing around, she grabbed her sweaty shirt from the floor and ran it under the faucet quickly. She scrubbed the toothpaste off the counter and wiped the hairs out of the sink. She scooped up her running clothes and tossed them into the hamper in her bedroom, which didn't look half bad.

"Phew. Sorry about that. I'm just going to drop this into the trash chute down the hall. Are you okay for half a minute? Help yourself to the kitchen. I at least have water."

Marjorie laughed as Cari trotted down the hallway to the chute. She tossed the garbage bag through the door and returned to her apartment just as her phone started ringing. *Genevieve, finally!*

"Tell me that you found that kid!"

"I did. We brought him over to the station."

"We?"

"I pulled my partner in. We are just getting ready to speak with him. We had planned to catch up with him tomorrow."

"What?"

"Oh, sorry. We're familiar with this guy. I can't tell you anymore right now, and I don't know how long this interview will take. I really wish we could speak with Marjorie first. How is she doing?"

"She calmed down once we got off campus and over to my apartment. I told her to help herself to the fridge's contents. I think she found some cheese and water and a banana."

"Five-star service right there. Okay, I can ask someone else to sit in on this interview if you think I should come over now; it's almost nine o'clock. How late is too late to check back in?"

Cari looked over at the sofa where Marjorie had been eating. The young woman was asleep. "Maybe you should just catch up with us tomorrow. I think she just crashed."

"Okay. I'll have a patrol car swing by your building periodically until I can get a better grasp of what's going on here.

What's your address?"

"I'm in building four of the new Ridgeway Apartments on Grand." She heard Genevieve scribbling on paper.

"Got it. Don't open the door unless you know for sure who it is on the other side. I still feel like I'm flying a little blind here, Cari. I'm sorry that I didn't believe your theory that the deaths were connected. Is there anything you can give me before I head into this interview?"

"First of all, I never open my door without knowing who's on the other side. Second, I can't compromise my source here. It's her story to tell. She ran from her roommate because her roommate broke her confidence. I can't exactly turn around and do that to her again."

Genevieve sighed. "Keep your phone on. I can't promise that my partner won't want to interview her tonight."

"Fine. I wouldn't recommend that method, but who am I to give directions? Keep me posted."

Cari went into her bedroom to try to call Bob again. It had been over an hour since she'd last tried. Maybe he had listened to her message. She hit *send* and crossed her fingers that he would answer.

"Cari, I probably shouldn't have answered this. You really crossed the line."

"Bob, I'm SO sorry. Ithaca's girlfriend called me and needed my help, so I just jumped up from my desk and left it unattended. It was careless of me. I'm sorry."

"But we were off the record, Cari! How could Cardian know what I said? Did you record me, Cari?! Why would you do that?"

Cari's head dropped. "I was completely out of line. I let my desire to get on the front page take the lead over what I knew was right. The recording was only so I could get the names correct for later, not because I was going to quote you in my article. I'm really sorry, Bob. I hope you don't get in trouble because of me."

"Luckily, my boss doesn't even *know* that Twitter exists, so he never saw it. I only found out because I heard the lieutenant yelling at one of the detectives in the precinct on my way out of the office tonight."

"That was probably my other friend getting into trouble on my account. Can you forgive me, Bob?"

He sighed. "I could never stay mad at you, Cari. We've been friends for too long."

"Thank you, Bob. I owe you this time. When this gets wrapped up, I'll get you some tacos from Larry's. As many as you want." She grinned into the phone.

"It's a d—deal." Bob stuttered. "Good luck with your article, Cari. See you around." He ended the call.

Cari exhaled. She had almost ruined one of her only friendships by trying to bend the rules to get ahead. Bob was too nice for her; she really didn't deserve his friendship.

Chapter 18

Andrew sat in a tiny room with what he knew was a fake mirror. He wished he had brought a jacket with him; it was freezing in here! He looked at his watch again. He'd been sitting in here for over half an hour already. They took his phone before they put him in the back of the detective's car. The old detective was such a grump. It was probably past his bedtime at this point. He had to be at least forty-five years old, maybe even fifty.

He drummed his fingers on the table. He wished he had his phone so he could call his coach or Wiley or his mom, anyone! He was starting to get hungry too in addition to being so cold. If he hadn't eaten dinner at 4:30 today, he would have been fine. He stared at the mirror, wondering if they were watching him. Today just kept getting worse and worse. The only good thing was that they had the powder back, but how was he going to pick his up if he was in here?

* * * * * * * * *

Genevieve watched the stocky, young man through the glass. She could tell that he was angry, but there was something else. He was nervous. He wasn't completely sure why they had brought him in and it was making him fidgety.

"What do you think, Alex? Have we let him squirm long enough?"

"Probably. Plus, it's getting late. I don't want to be here all night."

"What are you, eighty-five?"

"Not funny. I need my beauty rest."

"Don't I know it."

"Also not funny. C'mon, let's see what he has to say."

Genevieve followed Alex into the interrogation room. The young man's head popped up from the table when he heard the door open. He glared at her as she sat down in front of him. Alex stood in the corner and leaned against the wall.

Genevieve had a folder with the printouts from the app Niles had used to schedule the meeting with Delamont. She opened it and took out the top sheet of paper. She pretended to read its contents before looking him in the eye.

"Mr. Niles, do you know what this is?"

"I couldn't possibly."

"Detective." Alex grunted at him.

"What?" Niles asked.

"You couldn't possibly, Detective. Be respectful."

He rolled his eyes. "I couldn't possibly, Detective."

"It's a printout from a messaging program that allows its users to schedule meetings with their contacts that use the same app. Sound familiar?"

"Meetable?" He asked.

"That's the one." She smiled. "Funny thing. When my partner talked to you yesterday, you never mentioned scheduling a meeting with Dr. Delamont for early Saturday morning."

"He didn't ask."

Genevieve put her hand up before Alex could growl again. "You didn't think it was relevant to mention this to him?"

Niles shrugged.

"I didn't catch that. Yes, it wasn't relevant?"

"I canceled the request, so why would it be relevant, *Detective*?" He spat the last word out.

"You know what else is funny? Now, you can't find this on the app. It's only visible on the computer version, but you can see if you have a canceled meeting. *And* you can see what time your

186

Leslie A. Piggott

contact put in the cancellation. Isn't that funny, Mr. Niles?"

Niles started to shrug again, but his eyes flashed quickly when she mentioned the time stamp. "I don't hear you laughing, Detective."

"You're right. I'm not laughing. In fact, I'm really confused, Mr. Niles. Not only did you not mention having a meeting scheduled with a murder victim on the morning of said victim's murder, but you also failed to mention that you canceled it right around the same time he died or shortly thereafter. That makes me suspicious. What about you, Detective Runimoss?"

"It doesn't look good for him, Detective Viacorte. You know what? Here's what I think happened. I think Mr. Niles here was upset with our Dr. Delamont about something, so he requested a meeting. Dr. Delamont loved his athletes and never refused a meeting, so he accepted the request. Mr. Niles arrived to his meeting and got into an argument with Dr. Delamont. Did you know that Mr. Niles plays baseball for Onore University, Detective?"

"I think that came up at some point, Detective."

"I find it interesting that Mr. Niles plays baseball and also is the current record holder in home runs."

"That is interesting."

"He can probably swing a bat pretty damn hard."

"I bet you're right about that too."

Alex pushed off the wall and walked over to the table. Bending down to Niles' face, he spoke again in a whisper. "I bet he could really do some damage if he swung a trophy at someone's head, don't you think?"

Before Genevieve could respond, Niles pounded both palms onto the table. "Stop it! I wouldn't hurt Dr. D! You've got this all wrong. I never laid a hand on him."

"I'm all ears, Mr. Niles," Alex said, straightening up.

"You see, it's like this. I requested a meeting with Dr. D, like

187

you said. And, yes, he accepted it, but then when I arrived on Saturday morning and went to his office, I found him dead on the floor. I've never seen a dead body before. There was so much blood. I panicked. I ran back to my apartment and canceled the meeting. I didn't know the computer saved a record of that."

"Why wouldn't you have told us this? If you did nothing wrong, why the secrecy, Mr. Niles?" Genevieve asked.

"Just like you said, it looks really suspicious. Why would you believe me that I didn't kill him?"

"I don't know. Why would we believe you now? What proof do you have that you didn't kill him?"

"I only have my word. I didn't do it. I swear to you."

"Why were you meeting with Dr. D so early on a Saturday?"

"It was for the nutrition program. I had a couple of questions." He looked at his feet.

"I don't know, Detective. That sounds like a lie."

"It's the truth."

"Let's stick a pin that for now, shall we, Mr. Niles?"

"Why were you chasing a young woman across your college campus this evening?" Alex asked.

Niles slumped back in his chair, looking defeated. "I needed to ask her a question."

"The last person you had questions for ended up dead, Mr. Niles. What kinds of questions do you ask?"

"It's not like that! You're twisting my words!"

"Explain yourself, by all means."

Niles mumbled under his breath.

"I didn't catch that. It almost sounded like you said that you didn't want to." Genevieve raised her eyebrows.

A look of shock briefly flashed across the young man's face. "I think I want a lawyer. And I want to go home. You can't hold me here forever."

Genevieve stood up. "Do you know your lawyer's phone

Leslie A. Piggott

number? We can go get your phone and you can call him or her."
He shook his head. "I want to call my dad. He can get me a lawyer."
"We'll be back momentarily, Mr. Niles." Alex told him. He opened the door to the interrogation room and held it for Genevieve.
Once they were back in the adjacent room, Genevieve spoke to Alex. "I don't know that I see him as a murderer, Alex. He's rude, yes, and he's not telling us everything, but I don't think he's a killer."
"We've got his back against the wall. He knows it. That's why he asked for a lawyer."
"I don't know. Something is definitely off with his story, and I think it has to do with the young woman he was chasing tonight."
"The young woman that your friend is keeping at her apartment?"
Genevieve nodded. "So, what do we do with this kid? I don't know that we can keep—"
Alex's phone was ringing. "Detective Runimoss...yes...another one? Okay. We'll be there in ten minutes." He turned to Alex. "That was Officer Webb over at Onore University. They have another body: Dr. Bryan Hartfeld."

* * * * * * * * * *

Andrew sat in the interrogation room with another police officer. After the two detectives left to get his phone, all hell broke loose and it seemed like he'd been forgotten in the chaos. Then this officer came in with his phone and said that the detectives had to go see about another matter related to the case. At least he had his phone back.
His dad had asked why he needed a lawyer, but Andrew didn't know what to tell him. They weren't supposed to tell anyone about

189

the program or the supplement. He couldn't explain why he had been chasing that girl if he couldn't talk about the program. His dad had refused to help him and definitely wouldn't call a lawyer if Andrew couldn't even say why he needed one.

He was supposed to be picking up his next dose first thing in the morning, but it didn't seem like he was going to get out of here any time soon. Maybe he could ask one of the other athletes to grab his, especially now that they all knew each other. He sent a text to Wiley.

I got hung up with something, can u get my pickup 4 me

Sure man, where r u

Long story tell u later

Ok

Once they had all learned that the program was back on, half of the group felt like it would be okay to leave Ithaca's girlfriend alone. Andrew didn't agree. She was talking to reporters, making plans to talk to the police. They needed to get her to see how important it was to keep that info to herself. Emma agreed with him for once. No one knew where she was. She had jumped in that reporter's car and sped off into the night. He couldn't try to find out from the roommate either; she had stopped answering his texts. This was all such a nightmare! He was glad that he had decided to turn his phone off before getting pulled into the station for questioning. At least thirty messages had been exchanged while he was in this little room. The detectives surely would have been even more suspicious if his phone had been blowing up while they had it. He was stuck in this stupid room, freezing his ass off, and no one cared! He was about to pound his fist on the table when he remembered that his 'guard' was still with him. He grimaced instead.

"Am I gonna get out of here soon? You haven't even said why I'm being held."

"Not my call, chief."

"Please, I have class tomorrow and practice! I'm not going to run away or something."

"Again, not my call." He never even looked up from his crossword puzzle.

Andrew groaned and laid his head down on the table.

* * * * * * * * * *

Emma pursed her lips together. She hated to agree with that Niles kid, but he was right about this. If they didn't find out what the girlfriend knows, it could come back to bite them in a really bad way. Casey wanted to move on. She thought if they cooled it for a bit, people would forget, and things could go back to normal. Derek agreed with Casey. Bothering the girlfriend would just make her more suspicious and want to talk to the police more.

She scrolled back through the message thread. Andrew had been silent early on in the conversation. At one point, he had texted the group that he knew where Marjorie was ("the girl" as he always referred to her), but then they didn't hear from him again for a few hours. He was back to stating his opinion and trying to tell everyone what to do. She wondered why he had been silent for so long. It almost seemed like his phone had been off. Alan had asked earlier if Andrew had caught up with Marjorie, but Andrew didn't respond. She didn't think he had just overlooked the message. She thought he was choosing to deliberately not answer it. *We'll see about that, Niles.* She sent a message just to him.

Where were u earlier? Why did u stop messaging?

She tapped her foot while she waited for him to respond. Luckily, he had an iPhone too, so she could see that he had read the message. He would have to respond now or look even more suspicious. Finally, a message popped up.

Got pulled over 4 speeding on campus

Speeding on campus? Emma had gotten her share of speeding

tickets in her short driving history. It was not an hours long experience. It was maybe a fifteen-to-twenty-minute experience. Did Niles think she was an idiot now or what?

And for the other 90 min...?

Had a mtg. Lay off

A meeting? Emma didn't believe that for a minute. Niles might have gotten pulled over for speeding, but that wasn't the end of the story. Emma felt certain that he'd been questioned further by the police. He was making this worse for all of them. She decided the rest of the group needed to know and started a message without Niles. Even if he was on her side about Marjorie, he couldn't be trusted any longer. Who knows what he had told the police already?

* * * * * * * * * *

Genevieve let Alex drive over to Onore. She was still trying to process Hartfeld's murder. How did all of this fit together?

"What did Officer Webb tell you?"

"Hartfeld was found strangled in his hamster lab room by the cleaning crew. They arrived at nine o'clock and couldn't get the door to open the whole way. When they looked inside, they saw him on the floor and called 9-1-1. Dispatch switched it to campus police because he was on campus. Then Webb called us."

"Why does she think his death is related to Delamont's? I didn't realize that she knew they were friends."

"She most likely still doesn't know that. She just assumed that since we were already working one murder on campus, we should probably hear about the second one. I hate to say it, but I think your reporter friend is right. This is all tied together somehow."

Genevieve couldn't disagree. "There's definitely more to the story here. We're still short a few pieces of the puzzle, though."

Alex parked along the curb outside of the biology building.

Hartfeld had an office as well as a set of lab rooms inside the building. Genevieve looked up towards the building but didn't see anyone waiting to let them in.

"Is this the front of the building or the back?" She asked Alex.

"Hell if I know. Why?"

"I don't see anyone that's going to let us inside. We might have to walk around to a different entrance."

Alex stopped mid-stride. "When we asked for the ID numbers of people who had entered the gym on Saturday morning, did they give us the info for *all* of the doors or just that front one? I assumed the badge entry feature was only found on the front entrance. What if there were multiple entry points?"

"We can check with Officer Webb when we see her. I still don't see anyone over here. Should I call her or do you want to just walk around to the other side?"

Alex responded by stomping off towards what Genevieve viewed as the back of the building. She jogged to catch up. That was one way to answer her question. When they turned the corner, they saw Officer Cravits waiting by a set of double doors. Now that she could see this side of the building, Genevieve realized her assumption was incorrect. A bronze statue of a man holding his hat sat squarely in front of the building. Genevieve stopped to study it briefly. The plaque at the base of the statue read, "John Burke – a man of unquestionable integrity." There was also a summary that referred to Mr. Burke as *Honest John* and stated that *Onore University* was founded in tribute to this honorable man and that all its students and alumni were called to live with the honor and integrity exhibited by him. *Interesting,* she thought. She had always wondered where the university got its name.

"Are you coming or what?" Alex snapped her thoughts back to reality.

"Sorry! I was just reading about the statue. Did you know that *Onore* was founded in honor of this man?"

"Do we really need a history lesson right now, Gen?"

"I just thought it was interesting, you big Scrooge. I'm coming."

Officer Cravits held the door for them as they entered the building. The hallways were fairly dark as only every third ceiling panel light was powered on at this time of night.

"Are you a history buff, Detective Viacorte?" Officer Cravits asked her.

"Oh, not really. I just found that statue rather striking and wanted to know who it was. I don't think I've heard of John Burke before."

"Most people in this part of the country probably haven't, unless they go to school here. That's one of the tenants of the university: *honor*. The admissions committee requires every applicant to write an essay about what it means to be honorable and have integrity. Anyone who has a dishonorable past isn't even considered for admission."

Alex grunted as they stepped off the elevator. Officer Webb was waiting for them at the end of the hallway. She waved in recognition. Alex turned to Officer Cravits before the elevator doors closed.

"The ME and CSU team will be along shortly, so you'll need to let them in as well."

He nodded his understanding. Genevieve followed Alex down the hallway to Officer Webb. She was standing outside of a room labeled 'Hartfeld—animal research area'.

"This was Dr. Hartfeld's hamster lab. We called his lab manager already. She is on her way here now. We've also requested that the other members of his lab come in for interviews with you. A few of them have arrived and are waiting in the conference room around the corner."

Genevieve put on gloves and booties before entering the lab room. Inside, she saw a wall of cages housing at least thirty hamsters. A logbook sat on the counter across from the cages. Dr. Hartfeld was on the floor with his legs straight out. His eyes were still open, staring blankly up at the ceiling. Around his neck, she could see some dark red and purple bruising that seemed to be indicative of strangulation. Alex was already squatting down near the body. She stepped in for a closer look.

"Looks like some petechial hemorrhaging in his eyes, see here?" He pointed at both eyes. Genevieve nodded.

"Seems like a clear case of strangulation. I could see the bruising on his neck from the doorway." She turned to Officer Webb. "Please tell me that this building has cameras or an electronic entry log of some sort."

"You're in luck. It has both, depending on the entrance."

"We're going to need a copy of that footage. And speaking of multiple entrances, does the gymnasium have multiple ways to enter after hours, or does everyone have to go through the front doors?"

"There is a second entrance, but you have to have a key to get in there. It's always locked from the outside. Even when someone uses a key to unlock it, it doesn't stay unlocked. It's a security feature until we get the cameras and the badge entry system set up on that side."

"Do you have a list of everyone with a key?"

Officer Webb sighed. "Possibly, but because they aren't digital, we have no way of knowing who has made a copy for a friend or colleague. It's on the list to tighten up the security; we're just really behind. It hasn't been a priority because it's never needed to be a priority. Obviously, all of that has changed this week."

"Okay, which entrance has video here and which one uses electronic badge entry?"

"Both have badge entry, but the front entrance also has a camera. I'll get all of that to you shortly."

"I don't know what time classes start here tomorrow, but this floor will be off limits until CSU is finished," Alex interjected. "If there are lecture halls or labs that meet on this floor, they will need to be moved elsewhere."

"We already contacted the dean of the school to let her know that another death had occurred on campus. She is drafting a message that will be distributed to the student body and all of Onore's staff later tonight."

Alex nodded. "CSU will dust for prints in here, but I don't see a lot of evidence for them to collect. Hopefully, the killer was caught on camera or with his badge. We also need a roster of all the students in Hartfeld's classes. Until we get a better idea of what's going on here, everyone is considered a person of interest."

Before Officer Webb could respond, the ME stuck his head in the door. "I'm here with CSU. Can we get started, or do you need to look around some more?"

Alex shook his head no. "Go right ahead. The sooner we have a time of death, the sooner we can start eliminating potential suspects. Also, where is the victim's office?"

"Right this way," Officer Webb said as she pointed to her left.

Genevieve and Alex pulled off their gloves and booties when they were back in the hallway. They followed Officer Webb down a long hallway. She stopped in front of the second to last door and pulled out her key ring again, flipping through the keys one by one.

"Here we go," she said, unlocking the office.

"I can't believe you know which key unlocks every door on campus." Genevieve commented.

"There's a master key for every building. It unlocks every office and closet. Each building has a number, so I just have to remember which number goes with which building." She smiled. "I need to check in with the dean, so I'll leave you here. Just pull the door closed when you're finished. I can unlock it for CSU again later if they need access after you're gone."

Hartfeld's office was a bit messy, but it didn't look like anyone had searched it. An open laptop sat on the desk, but the screen was dark. Pulling his gloves back on, Alex touched the space bar lightly to wake it up. A password prompt appeared on the screen.

"Whatdya wanna bet it's *hamsters?*" He asked Genevieve.

She shrugged. "Try it, though it seems like the university would require something more stringent."

Alex typed in the word and hit enter. The prompt disappeared, revealing a paused video. Dr. Hartfeld's face was frozen on the screen. Alex glanced at Genevieve and then hit play. She hoped that it wasn't something that would self-delete after one view.

Hartfeld's voice filled the room as his face came into focus. "If you're watching this, then I'm probably dead or close to it. I don't know who is after me, but I can tell you one thing. I killed John…"

* * * * * * * * * *

Cari woke up to her cell phone ringing. Checking the screen, she saw that it was Bob calling. She swiped across quickly to answer it before it went to voicemail.

"Hey, Bob, what's up?"

"Were you asleep? Oh man, I'm sorry."

"It's fine. Don't worry about it. What's going on?"

"I just got called into another murder scene. It's at the university too. Guy's name was Bryan Hartfeld."

Cari sat up in bed. "Did you say Hartfeld?"

"Yeah, do you know him?"

"I've interviewed him! He is, I mean, was, well, weird. Something was not quite right with that guy."

"Well, there's a lot more wrong now. Someone strangled him earlier tonight. I gotta go. Don't use my name, okay, Cari?"

"No problem, Bob. I'm pretty surprised that you'd call me with information again after what happened earlier."

"It seems like you're the only one pushing this case in the right direction. I meant it when I said that I forgave you, Cari."

"Thanks, Bob. That means a lot."

Cari threw her covers back and got out of bed. She opened the door and saw that Marjorie was still asleep on the sofa. Glancing at her watch, she saw it was just before ten o'clock. No wonder Bob was so surprised that she was asleep. *Granny Cari, at your service*, she thought.

She had found Hartfeld to be really suspicious. Now he was dead too. Genevieve had to believe her theory at this point. Cari thought about calling her but figured that she was probably still at the crime scene and wouldn't answer. She pulled out her notebook and started writing down names and making connections with lines. She put Delamont in the middle of the page and drew a circle around his name. Then she drew an arrow away from that and wrote Ithaca. She wrote "Hartfeld" off to the other side and drew another arrow towards his name from Delamont's.

Cari was certain that the powder that Delamont was giving to Ithaca was not only the cause of Ithaca's death but also related to Delamont's murder. Hartfeld was a researcher in addition to teaching courses at the school. How did he fit in? Cari tapped her eraser on the page. The man had been adamant that his supplement was not tested on humans. He had even gotten angry about it. But what if Delamont had somehow gotten his hands on the supplement and given it to the athletes?

She turned on her laptop and started drafting a story. It was still all conjecture at this point, but she knew her editor would run with it if Cari could confirm the facts. To do that, she'd have to convince Genevieve to share some information with her.

Chapter 19

Genevieve rubbed her eyes in exhaustion. The last two days were starting to take a toll on her. She looked over at Alex who was gulping down yet another cup of coffee. She tried to shake the tiredness out of her head.

"Okay, let's review what we know." She walked over to the whiteboard behind them. Photos of Delamont and Hartfeld were held in place with little magnets. Off to the side, they had written the names of the athletes, Curtis Whitham, and Marjorie Pryor. Marjorie's name had a question mark next to it. Next to Whitham's name, she had written *financial problems*. Niles' name had an arrow going from it to Marjorie's with another question mark above it. She drew another arrow from Hartfeld to Delamont.

"Well, we learned a lot from that video," Alex said slowly. "That was one crazy guy."

Genevieve shuddered a bit. In the video, Hartfeld had confessed to murdering Delamont after the sports medicine doctor had gone to him for help regarding the nutritional supplement. Delamont had called Hartfeld in a panic after Ithaca's death. He admitted to taking the powder from Hartfeld's lab over several months while he was caring for the hamsters. Hartfeld observed that his friend was remorseful for stealing and betraying their friendship, but he was too enraged to forgive him. The project was never intended to be studied in humans. Obviously, it wasn't safe. Plus, humans were too greedy and too performance driven to see his study for its ingenuity. They would quickly become fixated on its *potential* to create super athletes.

Delamont had mentioned to Hartfeld that one of his athletes had requested an appointment for the following morning. He told his friend that he'd brought the powder home and would return it to him the following day. He had suggested that he join him for dinner on Saturday night, but Hartfeld couldn't wait. He already knew about the early meeting and decided to get there first. He entered the gym from the back entrance and waited outside Delamont's office. When his friend arrived, his anger renewed. If the police discovered that the kid had been using his supplement, he'd lose his job and all of his research would end! He forced Delamont into his office and grabbed the first thing he saw—the diving trophy—and swung it at Delamont's head. Immediately horrified, he wiped the trophy with his shirt to remove his fingerprints but left the blood on the small stars. He hadn't touched anything else in the office, so he quickly left and hoped that no one would see him exiting the building.

From there, he drove over to Delamont's house to retrieve his precious supplement. He knew where the extra key was hidden and let himself in. The container with the powder was sitting on the kitchen counter. He grabbed it and left the house, locking the door behind him. Hartfeld then told the camera that someone must have seen him leaving Delamont's house. Whoever that was had started trying to blackmail him.

Genevieve looked at the board again. "My money is on Whitham now. He wanted that powder back. Without the super athletes, his programs would start to lose, which would cost the school scholarship money. He was probably frantic to get that back." Her phone buzzed with a text. *Cari.*

"Who was that?" Alex asked. "Never mind. I agree, though, I want to talk to that Niles kid again. Did his lawyer ever show up?"

"No. Something about his dad not wanting to spend the money on it. He's in lockup right now. Probably really mad by this point. Without a lawyer, we still can't talk to him. I'm not sure if he wants a court-appointed attorney or not." She paused. "That was my friend, Cari. The girlfriend might know why Niles was chasing her. Why don't we bring her in and see what she can tell us?"

200

Alex frowned, then shrugged. "Fine, but I don't like working with reporters."

Genevieve called Cari. "Hey. Is your new friend awake, yet? I know it's early. Sorry…ok, great. Can you meet us at the station in half an hour? Perfect. See you soon." She ended the call.

"They're already awake and they'll be here in a few minutes."

* * * * * * * * * *

Cari pulled into the parking spot outside of the police station and looked over at Marjorie. "Are you sure you're up for this?"

She nodded. "Yes. I know Stephen really respected Dr. D. Regardless of how I feel about the man pushing what is effectively drugs onto students, he didn't deserve to die. Let's go talk to your friend and her partner."

Cari led Marjorie up the steps and into the precinct. Genevieve was waiting for them at the front desk. She gave them both visitor badges and walked them back to a conference room.

"Hi, Miss Pryor, my name is Detective Viacorte. This is my partner, Detective Runimoss. We just have a few questions for you this morning. Before we start, can we get you anything? Water? Coffee? I'd offer you a donut, but that's actually just a bad stereotype. I could send someone for a breakfast taco though?" She smiled.

"I'm fine, thanks. Ms. Turnlyle and I went by Starbucks already." She lifted the iconic cup at Genevieve.

"Oh, great! Okay, then, have a seat." Genevieve walked around to the other side of the table and sat down next to her partner while Cari and Marjorie sat down.

"Yesterday evening, a young man was chasing you across campus. That man's name is Andrew Niles. Are you familiar with him?"

"Yes, I mean, no. Not really. My roommate went on a date with him yesterday. She thought he was nice and was really touched that he had expressed concern for me since Stephen had died. As you know, I got spooked by you seeing the athlete at the restaurant last night, so I asked Ms. Turnlyle to take me home.

"I let my roommate know that I was home and then decided to soak in a bubble bath to try to relax. It seemed like everything was happening at once and I just wanted a little break, you know? But then my roommate called and we talked. I ended up telling her about Stephen and the powder, but I never thought she would tell someone else. I heard her come into the apartment and she was on the phone. She told the person on the line everything that I'd said! It was that guy—you said that his name was Andrew? Yeah, she told him what I said and I don't know why that scared me so much, but it did. I just took off and told her not to open the door to anyone. Thankfully, Ms. Turnlyle got there when she did."

"Let's back up for a second. This powder you mentioned, where did Stephen get it?"

"From Dr. D. He told me that it was something he took once a month. He was adamant that it wasn't steroids, but it all sounded weird to me. Is that what killed him?"

Genevieve glanced at her partner who nodded. "Miss Pryor—"

"Please, just call me Marjorie."

"Okay. Marjorie. The scientist who developed the powder never imagined that it would be given to humans. He developed it to try to understand some kind of metabolic pathway that is beyond my biology knowledge. He studied it in hamsters. The hamsters that received it had more stamina and more speed. Dr. Delamont learned about this through his friendship with the scientist and decided that giving it to some of his star athletes couldn't hurt anything. He did this without the scientist's knowledge. Unfortunately, the supplement wasn't safe for anyone with an underlying condition."

"But Stephen was healthy! He always passed the athletic physical; he was never sick!" Marjorie cried.

"We haven't been able to confirm this yet, but the scientist is speculating that Stephen had something called—" Genevieve checked her notes. "*Rhabdomyolysis.* It has to do with what happens when you overwork your muscles and they start to break down. Honestly, I don't understand it at all."

"I want to talk to him," Marjorie stated adamantly.

"You want to talk to...? Genevieve asked.

"The scientist. I want to talk to him."

"Unfortunately, that isn't possible. He was killed last night."

Marjorie grew pale. Cari's eyes widened. "You're saying...?"

Genevieve nodded. "His death is definitely related to these other two. I think we're narrowing down the suspect list. Are you sure we can't get you some water, Marjorie?"

She shook her head slowly as tears dropped off her cheeks and onto the table. "I just want to go home."

Cari reached for the young woman's hand and gave it a squeeze before releasing it. She looked at Genevieve and raised her eyebrows questioningly. "What do you think?"

"Miss Pryor—Marjorie. I would rather you stay here until we get a few more things squared away. I'm not sure who else might be looking for you and I want you to be safe." Genevieve responded.

Marjorie's shoulders sagged. "Fine. I have class at ten. Can I at least go to my classes?"

"We'll talk about it. For now, my partner and I need to go speak to someone else. Hang tight, okay?"

Chapter 20

Alex and Genevieve started down the hallway when they heard footsteps behind them. Glancing over their shoulders, they saw Cari hurrying after them. They turned around and waited for her.

"I'm sorry to interrupt, but I just wanted to ask a question."

"Shoot," Alex said to her.

"I don't want to hurt your investigation. I may not be a front-page journalist yet, but I am familiar with how the police prefer to handle the media."

"This doesn't sound like a question."

"Let her finish, Alex." Genevieve rebuked him.

"What I'm trying to ask is…can I get an exclusive? I have been following this since day one—since Ithaca collapsed. You wouldn't have known these deaths were related without me."

Alex grunted and maybe snorted too, but Genevieve spoke first. "We understand where you're coming from Cari. I'm not saying no, okay? We'll do what we can. That's the best I can offer."

Alex glared at her and started walking down the hallway again. Genevieve smiled at her friend and then turned to follow her partner. She knew that Cari was the newspaper's sportswriter and wondered how she was going to get control of this story before their lead reporter took it. She shook the thought from her head, reminding herself to focus on the problems at hand. She joined Alex at their desks.

"Okay, so this Niles kid was chasing the girlfriend for one of two reasons: one, he wanted to know if she had told anyone else about the powder and or two, he wanted to know specifically who she had told about the powder."

"We're now assuming that this powder is the nutritional supplement, right?" Alex asked.

"I think that's a fair assumption." She wrote powder above the arrow connecting Hartfeld and Delamont. "Clearly, the athletes in the program don't want it to end. They would lose their advantage."

"Right. We know Hartfeld took out Delamont, but who strangled Hartfeld?" He pulled up the images from the crime scene on his computer. "Look at the bruising on his neck. Whoever did this has large hands. I think we can rule out the four females unless you remember one of them having man hands."

Genevieve gave him the side eye. "I agree; the bruising was made by a man, not a woman. Also, Hartfeld was reasonably tall, so whoever did this would need to be a certain height to get the right leverage."

"Unless Hartfeld was bent over with his hamsters when it happened."

"What was the time of death? Did the ME send us his report yet?"

Alex clicked around on his computer. "Got the initial results. Time of death was between 5:30 and 6:00 in the evening. What time was our young friend chasing down co-eds on campus?"

Genevieve looked at her call history to see what time Cari had called her the night before. "It was right around eight o'clock. I don't think we can rule Mr. Niles out for this unless he can give us an alibi."

"We need to check Hartfeld's phone record and see who was harassing him. He said in the video that he was getting texts from an unknown number. Will the cell phone company be able to provide a number that was made hidden?"

"I hope so. It seems likely that whoever was bothering Hartfeld is our murderer."

* * * * * * * * *

Cari's phone buzzed with an incoming call. *Ollaman!* She should probably answer it away from Marjorie, but she didn't want to leave the young woman alone again. She swiped her thumb across the screen and answered the call.

"Mr. Ollaman! What can I do for you today?"

"*Miss Turnlyle*," he spat her name out. "I was just informed that there has been *another death* on the Onore campus."

"Sir?" Cari asked timidly.

"I have also been informed that *your car* was spotted at the police station this morning. I can't imagine why my *star* sportswriter would be at the police station. Are they having a corn hole tournament or something, my dear?" He asked sarcastically.

"Sir, I can explain."

"I'm waiting."

Cari took a deep breath and let it out slowly. She only had one chance to get this right. "You see, sir. Last Friday at the track meet, one of the runners collapsed in the middle of the race. I thought it seemed suspicious, so I looked into it some more. One thing led to another and I've kind of found myself in the middle of a big investigation, sir. I know you asked me to stay out of Cardian's way. I did not intend to overstep my bounds; I was just following the leads as they came."

"Last night you asked me to take down a tweeter thing, what? My wife says it's a tweet. Fine, a tweet that Cardian had posted on the internet. Fine, on Twitter. Stop interrupting me, Woman! Am I to believe that Cardian took that from you? The last time he talked to me, he didn't have a single lead on the Delamont case. How did you come to connect these dots when my veteran reporter could not?"

"Sir? Well, you see, honestly, some of it was luck. If I hadn't been covering that track meet on Friday, I wouldn't have seen Mr. Ithaca—" she glanced at Marjorie, suddenly remembering that she wasn't the only one in the room. "Mr. Ithaca collapse and, unfortunately, die. My gut told me that it wasn't really natural causes and the police have confirmed that sir. I'm hoping to have the whole story for you soon. I understand if you want me to turn my notes over to Lionel. He is the lead reporter after all." She held her breath.

"Turn your notes? What? You are a nice young lady, but you have to take the reins when they are handed to you! This is your story. Run with it. Keep me posted. I'll take care of Lionel." He ended the call.

Cari let out her breath. She had fully expected her boss to give her another lecture on knowing her place. She blinked, wondering if the conversation had really happened. Before she could pinch herself, she heard a sniffle come from Marjorie.

"Oh, Marjorie! I didn't mean for—"

"It's okay, Cari. You are a good person. I can see that. I know this story means a lot to you, but I have also seen you spring into action to help someone you hardly know just because she asked. You might not know this, but our school, *Onore University* is all about honor. It's one of the founding tenants of the school. You have to have a background of integrity and honor or they won't even look at your application. You deserve to tell this story. It won't be a proud moment for Onore, but it is a story that needs to be told."

Cari was shocked by the kindness and fortitude the young woman was showing her. "Thank you so much. Your words mean a lot to me. I will do my best to honor Stephen's memory in my article."

Marjorie looked at her watch. "I should probably call Stephen's parents and give them an update. Do you think the detectives are going to have the medical examiner check to see if he has that Rhabdo-whatever-disease?"

"They might have already done it. I'll make a note to ask when they come back."

* * * * * * * * * * *

Genevieve sat in the interview room with another young athlete. He had short, blonde hair and brown eyes. He was slumped in his chair and his face was downcast.

"Mr. Debony, do you know why we brought you in this morning?"

He looked around the room, like the answer might be written on one of the walls. "I'm guessing it's because of Dr. Hartfeld. I saw an announcement that he was dead and so my biochemistry class was canceled today. I don't know why I'm the only student of his here, though."

"Mr. Debony, did you ask Dr. Hartfeld to meet you at his office yesterday?"

"I did, but he wasn't there to let me in! I waited for fifteen minutes in the cold!" He looked off to the corner of the room.

Genevieve looked at him quizzically. "You can't enter the building with your school ID?"

"That only works at the gym. You have to be a GTA, uh, a graduate teaching assistant, or a professor to get into the regular buildings on the weekends." He shrugged.

"So, you never saw Dr. Hartfeld yesterday afternoon?"

"What? No! Wait. Do you think I killed him? What are you, crazy?" He sat upright in his chair.

"I'll be asking the questions, Mr. Debony."

"Fine." He shrugged again and slumped back into his chair.

"What can you tell me about AD Whitham?"

"AD…oh, Coach Whitham? I mean, he's okay. I don't know him very well."

"I think you know him better than most athletes, isn't that right?"

"What? Oh man. Is he dead too?" Debony moaned.

"No, Mr. Debony. AD Whitham is alive and, well, he's alive." She stopped short of saying more.

"Then what do you mean, I knew him better?"

Genevieve pulled out two sheets of paper from the file in front of her. "You have been calling and texting AD Whitham quite extensively over the last two days." She set the two sheets in front of him.

"He was calling me too! And what's wrong with that?"

"Why did your athletic director need to communicate with you so heavily over this past weekend?"

Debony looked to the corner of the room again. "We had a problem with our nutrition program."

"Ah, yes. The infamous nutrition program. Well, Mr. Debony, you can cut the crap. I know all about your little program. The protein supplement, the, uh, powder as you call it, has been found and will no longer be distributed to any students."

Debony's eyes grew wide. "You can't do that! There's nothing wrong with it. It's just a supplement. It's not illegal."

"Not yet. Now, you were saying about AD Whitham?"

Debony sighed. "I didn't have a choice! He's in charge of all the scholarships! I NEED my scholarship. I didn't lay a hand on Hartfeld. I wouldn't do that, no matter who was asking me to."

Chapter 21

C ari looked out the little window in the conference room door when she caught movement from the corner of her eye and heard a commotion in the hallway. Detective Runimoss was marching AD Whitham down the hallway in handcuffs. *AD Whitham?!* Whitham's face was growing redder by the second and she could hear him shouting at the detective.

"You're making a mistake! Think about how this is going to hurt the university, the students, all the programs—you're ruining it for everyone!"

Marjorie had joined her and was trying to peer out the window too. Cari was about to open the door and start asking questions when the door opened and Genevieve walked inside.

"Hey Cari. It took some convincing, but you got it. You get the story. We're holding back the news conference until this afternoon so that you can get the exclusive." She handed Cari a file. "This isn't the *whole* story, but it's what the department is willing to share."

"Genevieve, wow! I can't believe it." She looked at Marjorie. "Is it safe for her to leave and go to class and all that now?"

Genevieve nodded. "You're welcome to stay and hear the rest of the story first, if you want."

Marjorie nodded. "That would be great, thanks."

"Let's see. Where should I start? You already know some of the story. After Dr. Hartfeld killed Dr. Delamont, he started getting mysterious texts from an unknown number. They grew increasingly hostile, which led him to make a video telling us his side of the story. He left that on his laptop. Unfortunately, he didn't know who was harassing him; he just knew why. The person had seen him leaving Delamont's house with a package of the powder that Dr. Delamont gave to the athletes. They wanted it back.

"We were able to get Hartfeld's phone records and found out who was behind the unknown number. Unfortunately, sending menacing texts doesn't prove that the person was our murderer. However, another person had been in contact with Hartfeld too. One of his students, who was also one of the athletes in Delamont's program, had requested help with the biochemistry course Hartfeld taught. On the surface, that seemed innocent enough, but in a case laced with coincidences, we couldn't overlook it.

"We brought both the student and Whitham in for questioning. Luck did not favor the bold today. AD Whitham was spotted by the student leaving the biochemistry building. Shortly after that, the athletes were informed that the powder had been recovered and the program was back on. We found the powder in Whitham's office after we executed a search warrant.

I'm sorry if you missed your class this morning, Marjorie. I'm sure your professors will understand, though. Can I give you a ride somewhere?"

Marjorie looked from Genevieve to Cari and back again. "Actually, Stephen's parents are on their way up here now. As you probably know, they are finally going to let them have his body. They just have to fill out some paperwork and then the mortuary can do whatever they do. Thank you, Detective Viacorte. What is going to happen with this powder now? Are you sure that you got it all back?"

Genevieve nodded. "We contacted each of the student athletes. No one has any left. They are all being screened for *Rhabdomyolysis* as well as some other conditions that Dr. Hartfeld's colleagues have suggested. They will be monitored over the course of the next two to three months to make sure no one has any damage that's gone undetected."

Marjorie's phone chimed with a message. "That's Stephen's parents, so I need to go. I don't know what to say except thank

211

you." She shook Genevieve's hand and gave Cari a hug.

Genevieve watched her walk down the hallway before turning back to Cari. "Listen, Cari. I'm sorry again for not taking your theory more seriously at the beginning."

Cari waved her off. "No, no need to apologize. I show up out of the blue after years of radio silence and try to worm my way into your case. You were just doing your job. However," she paused and turned her head sideways. "That doesn't mean that we can't do a better job of staying in touch. Who knows? Maybe this will become a regular thing, me helping you solve cases."

Genevieve started to frown. "Now, Cari, you know—"

"I'm just saying, let's not close the door on this. We work well together, don't you think?" She smiled. "I need to go chat with my boss. Thank you for this." She waved the folder at Genevieve.

"Thank you, Cari. Good luck with your story."

Cari stepped forward and gave Genevieve a hug. While she was grateful for the story, she was also happy to have reconnected with her friend. Even if Genevieve didn't want to include Cari in her investigations, they could still make time for their friendship. *Speaking of friendships,* Cari thought. She needed to give Stephen's roommate a call before the story broke.

Epilogue

"Cari, my dear! I hadn't heard from you and was starting to think I needed to send out the search party."

"Hi, Grandmother. I'm sorry for being out of touch the last few days. A lot has happened. I'm not even sure where to start."

"Well, start with how your name ended up on the front-page story on Tuesday morning!"

Cari grinned. "I thought you might have seen that. I was probably more shocked than anyone, well, maybe not Lionel! My editor realized that I wasn't the one trying to steal someone's story; I was the one really trying to chase the story. After Lionel snooped through my workstation, I had to smooth things over with Bob too. He thought that I had been using our friendship to get ahead in my career."

"And?" Her grandmother asked after a lengthy pause.

"If I'm being honest, I was. I wanted that story so badly that I was overlooking what really mattered. Thankfully, Bob showed me mercy and is still speaking to me. It took a little groveling and several breakfast tacos to get him to come around."

Her grandmother laughed. "Oh, Cari. You're always up to something. I'm glad you apologized and worked things out with Bob. He's a nice young man and a good...friend."

"Now, Grandmother, don't you go getting ideas." Cari laughed. "Bob and I are just friends."

"Okay, my dear. I'm proud of you. You worked hard and did a good job with your story. I bought an extra copy of your paper this week so that I could cut your article out and hang it on my fridge. I showed it to all of my book club friends yesterday, and they were so impressed. I'm proud of you, girl!"

"Thank you, Grandmother. I should let you go. I love you."
"I love you more."

Thank you for reading *Chasing the Edge*. If you enjoyed the book, please take a moment to leave a brief review.
To learn more about the characters from this book and stay up to date on future books in the series by visiting my website: https://leslieapiggott.com.

Acknowledgments

This is a work of fiction. None of the characters are real.

Shout out to my editor, Jennie Rosenblum for making my story come to life. Thank you for all your advice and guidance.

Thank you to Danielle Johnston for a lovely cover image. It is so nice to be able to send someone a sketch of an idea and see it cleaned up so beautifully.

To Lisa and all of the Indies United group: thank you for your support, advice, and expertise!

About the Author

Leslie A. Piggott lives in the Austin, Texas area with her husband and their two children. She is a scientist-turned-mom who received her doctorate in Biomedical Sciences from the University of Texas Health Science Center at Houston. In addition to writing, she also enjoys running marathons, quilting, knitting, singing in the church choir, and watercolor painting. She has previously published two watercolor and poetry books, both in 2021: *Poems in the Pandemic*, and *Art in Words*. Her first novel, *Rising Pressure* was published in January of 2022. To sign up for her newsletter, you can visit her website at https://leslieapiggott.com.

www.ingramcontent.com/pod-product-compliance
Lightning Source LLC
Chambersburg PA
CBHW011516100726
47899CB00010BD/3387

* 9 7 8 1 6 4 4 5 6 4 9 1 2 *